LESLIE McFARLANE'S HOCKEY STORIES
VOLUME 2

LESLIE McFARLANE'S
HOCKEY STORIES
VOLUME 2

EDITED BY BRIAN McFARLANE

KEY PORTER BOOKS

Library and Archives Canada Cataloguing in Publication

McFarlane, Leslie, 1902–1977
    Leslie McFarlane's hockey stories / edited by Brian McFarlane.

ISBN 1-55263-717-4 (v. 1).—ISBN 1-55263-848-0 (v. 2)

    1. Hockey stories, Canadian (English) I. McFarlane, Brian, 1931–
II. Title. III. Title: Hockey stories.

PS8525.F4L48 2005   jC813'.54   C2005-902769-X

The publisher gratefully acknowledges the support of the Canada Council for the Arts and the Ontario Arts Council for its publishing program. We acknowledge the support of the Government of Ontario through the Ontario Media Development Corporation's Ontario Book Initiative.

We acknowledge the financial support of the Government of Canada through the Book Publishing Industry Development Program (BPIDP) for our publishing activities.

Key Porter Books Limited
Six Adelaide Street East, Tenth Floor
Toronto, Ontario
Canada M5C 1H6

www.keyporter.com

Text design: Ingrid Paulson
Electronic formatting: Marijke Friesen

Printed and bound in Canada

06 07 08 09 10 5 4 3 2 1

CONTENTS

FOREWORD

AS A YOUNG LAD growing up in Northern Ontario, my father, Leslie McFarlane, witnessed some of the greatest hockey players in the world demonstrate their skills in Cobalt and Haileybury when those two towns held franchises in a unique league called the National Hockey Association.

When the pro teams folded, fans followed the senior and junior amateur teams. My father would recall those games, especially the battles between bitter rivals Sudbury and Sault Ste. Marie, as the most exciting action on ice he'd ever seen.

"Some of those amateur stars were good enough to play with any pro club," he told me once, "and in time, a lot of them did.

"To see Bill Cook or Shorty Green thread their way through a barricade of swinging sticks, to see Babe Donnelly wind up behind his net and go zigzagging down the ice to draw the goalie out and slam the puck into the net was to see hockey at its thrilling best."

As a young reporter at the *Sudbury Star*, he wrote about those games and interviewed the players.

It wasn't long before my father called on his creative juices to write about fictional players and their exploits and challenges. And he found a market for his yarns in the pulp magazines of the day.

I managed to collect most of his action-packed stories and store them away. Now I'm delighted to present them to a new generation of fans.

Let's set the scene for some long-ago action. The old barn is packed and the fans are howling for the game to begin. The referee rings a hand bell and the players take their positions. Each team has just two substitutes on the bench because sixty-minute men are common. The fur-coated goal judges slip and slide along the ice and take up their positions behind the net, knowing they risk being bowled over by incoming forwards going hell-for-leather after the bouncing puck.

The forwards glare at each other and whack sticks as they move in for the opening face off. The puck is thrown in. The game—and the book—are underway.

—Brian McFarlane

STANLEY CUP JITTERS

YOUNG BUD PORTER stormed recklessly into a corner after the puck. A red-shirted defenceman was half a jump ahead of him, but Bud Porter was in the frame of mind to argue the right of way with a freight train. He pelted in, regardless, as thirteen thousand fans screamed with delight. When the defenceman nailed him with an elbow, he veered as if he had been sideswiped by a moving van. He skidded into the backboards with a walloping crash. It sounded like a man falling off a scaffold and bringing the framework down after him. Bud uncoiled himself, knelt thoughtfully on hands and knees for a second, gave his head a shake, reached for his stick and got up on his skates again.

"G'wan back to the bench, you dumb lug!" screeched a red-haired female behind the screen.

"Yeah, you clumsy dope!" piped her escort. "Tell your old man to send out a hockey player."

Bud swayed groggily. The net was jumping and bobbing

in front of him, the ice surface was doing a shimmy, and the boards seemed to surge back and forth as if ready to take another whack at him.

The Reds were ganging the Blue goal. Bud pitched into the melee and pounced on Renault, his check. He tried to block Renault out of the play, sparred with him, pushed him around. The puck flew out from a struggling knot of players. Renault's stick flashed toward it, but Bud was nearer. He took a whack at the rubber, trying to bat it out into the clear, down the ice.

He was in too much of a hurry. The puck skimmed out in front of the net, hit a skate, deflected. It just missed the post. Another inch or so, and it would have gone into the open side of the net. The crowd screeched, then sank back gasping. The Blue goalie almost had heart failure. A defenceman scooped the puck over the glass and the whistle blew. Fresh troops came tumbling out onto the ice. Head down, Bud Porter skated back to the bench.

He slumped down, panting. His father, a big, grizzled man with sharp blue eyes under shaggy brows, said quietly, "Look before you shoot, son."

Bud sucked in deep breaths of air. He knew he had come within a hairbreadth of realizing the hockey player's nightmare—scoring against his own team. He was playing so hard, so anxious to make up for his poor showing thus far in the series, that he had simply banged at the puck without thinking.

He looked up at the clock. Five minutes to play in the third period. The Blues were trailing by one goal in the fifth game of the Stanley Cup series, already tied up at two games apiece.

"You're pressing too hard, son," said Amby Porter, manager of the Blues. "Take it easy, but watch for the breaks. Keep your head up when you shoot. You've seen Nels Stewart play. Looks lazy, doesn't he? But it doesn't show in the scoring averages. And he's outlasted plenty of guys who play their heads off and don't get anywhere."

Bud nodded. He had heard all this before. But, darn it all, when he got out there, he couldn't help giving all he had. This was serious hockey. A world title hung on these games. More than that. He had shown them that Amby Porter knew what he was doing in bringing his own son up from the minors. The sports writers had said plenty about it; said he wasn't ripe, wasn't good enough; that Amby Porter was letting parental enthusiasm run away with his better judgment.

"If we can tie it up," said Amby Porter quietly, "we'll take 'em in the overtime, sure. We're in better shape."

The Red machine, riddled by injuries in the early stages of the playoffs, was weak on reserves. It was telling against the Reds now. Amby Porter had been shooting his fresher men in there for a sustained series of smashing attacks in the past seven minutes.

It was like the savage final-round onslaught of a young, strong fighter against a smart, cagy old-timer who had already outpointed him, but whose legs were gone and who was covering up, stalling, clinching, trying to evade a storm of swift, sharp punches that were breaking past his faltering defence.

The Reds hung on. They checked with stick and body. Their goalie plunged and bobbed and kicked and dived. Players piled up in wild scrambles in the crease, struggled fiercely in the corners. The second hand of the big clock flicked around the face, the minute hand jumped notch by notch up the left-hand side. Four minutes. Three minutes! A desperate Red skied the puck down the ice and it rolled over the Blues' line. The whistle blew. Amby Porter hustled reserves off the bench.

"Go on, son. Keep your head up!"

Bud scrambled out. Amby Porter was throwing five forwards into the game in the final bid for that goal, and Bud had a feeling that they were going to get that goal, too. His dad was giving him a chance to be in on it, maybe to score it. That would be a great vindication of Amby Porter, if his own son tied up that game. The knockers would have to put away their hammers then.

The Red goalie pulled off three super-saves in a row. Bud Porter took a butt end from Renault that sent him sprawling. He scrambled to his feet again, about fifteen feet out, and just as he did so, the puck came skimming out from a tangle of players in a corner, clicked smartly against the blade of his stick. There wasn't a soul within checking distance. He had the goaltender at his mercy. The Red goalie crouched and then dived as Bud came rampaging in.

The goalie's headlong dive was short. There was the gaping, open net. All Bud Porter had to do was skate in and shove the rubber over the line. The tying goal! If he got it away before anyone reached him—

Bud Porter scooped at the puck, with the screams of the crowd ringing in his ears. He scooped at it blindly, frantically, hastily. And when it left his stick he looked up—looked up to see the puck taking a high, vicious course, up, up, just shaving over the top of the net and into the back screen. The goalie scrambled back into the cage. Thirteen thousand fans set up an outraged bellow of disappointment. And thirty seconds later the buzzer sounded with the score unchanged.

• • •

HIS TEAMMATES didn't have much to say about it, but their faces were grim. The fans had plenty to say. And so had the sports writers. Bud read a sample next morning:

Parental pride is all right in its place, but Amby Porter ought to wake up to the fact that it should have no place in masterminding a big-league hockey team during anything so important as a Stanley Cup series. Son Bud is a pretty fair hockey player—a promising youngster who will undoubtedly go far in the game—but he hasn't gone far enough yet.

It's as plain as the nose on Pa Porter's face that the kid isn't of Stanley Cup calibre; but, like the same nose, everybody seems to be able to see it except Pa Porter himself. He insisted on bringing the youngster up from the farm team over the heads of three boys who are considerably more experienced, and even if Master Bud is only a third stringer, his lack of seasoning has already been costly.

How he missed that open net in the final stages of last night's game, with the goalie helpless outside the crease, the puck at the end of his stick and not a Red within ten feet of him, will always remain a mystery to this disheartened critic.

Over-anxiety—just plain inexperience to you—was the answer, of course. There isn't a morsel of doubt that the Blues would have taken that precious fifth game if it had gone into overtime.

That missed goal may well have been the turning point of the entire series. The Reds need only one more game and they'll have home ice advantage in the final tilt if the series goes the limit. Around the Blue camp it is an open secret that as the series goes, so go Amby Porter's chances for a renewal of his contract.

Bud read that at the breakfast table next morning. He squinted across at his father. Amby Porter was drinking coffee with a preoccupied air, but he didn't seem worried. It was pretty hard to read Amby Porter's mind.

"Did you see this, Dad?"

Bud thrust the folded newspaper across the table, indicating the troublesome paragraph with his finger.

Amby Porter nodded shortly. "I saw it."

"I guess it's true, isn't it?"

"That part about over-anxiety is true enough. Honest, Bud, if you went down to the rink this morning and practiced trying to hoof that puck over the net from that angle and from that close in, I'll bet you couldn't do it—not if you tried for an hour."

Bud sat back in his chair. "I guess you'd better drop me, and bring up one of the other fellows from the farm team," he said.

"What's the matter? Not feeling well?"

"You know what's the matter, Dad. I'm not good enough. And you can't afford to fool around with anything so important as a Stanley Cup series," said Bud, unconsciously quoting from the article. "Why, it's liable to cost you your job."

Amby Porter took another sip of coffee. "I brought you up from the farm team and threw you into the series for two reasons, boy. One is that you're my son, and I want to see you make good in hockey in a big way. I never even got into a Cup series in all my playing career. So maybe we can put it down partly to sentiment. The other reason is that you're a hockey player."

"Lots of people don't seem to think so."

"Baloney. If you'd scored that goal, the newspaper boys would have been on the other side of the fence, cheering their heads off for you. That shot was about an inch out. Well, there's more than an inch difference between a hockey player and a dud. Even if you weren't my kid I'd have picked you from the farm team anyhow."

"You would?"

"Think I'm so dumb that I'd have thrown you into the series if you weren't good enough? Huh! I may be sentimental, but I'm not that sentimental."

"Yes, but I'm not good enough," insisted Bud stubbornly. "I get out there and I seem to forget all the hockey I ever learned."

"I know what's wrong with you."

"I'm too young."

"Get that idea out of your head. I can name you a score of stars who were top-notch players at twenty-one. Maybe they got better as they got older and picked up a few more tricks, but fellows like Morenz, Jackson, Joliat, the Cook brothers, Clancy—why, they were first-rate hockey players when they were scarcely out of short pants."

"You're classing me with them?"

"You've got natural ability in their class. You can skate, stickhandle, shoot, and pass. You've got hockey instinct. Your legs will never be better—one reason I brought you up. Older players have to save their legs. You don't tire now."

"If I'm as good as all that," said Bud bitterly, "we wouldn't have lost that game last night."

"You didn't lose it. Our defence let in three goals. Our forwards couldn't get more than two. You might have helped win it, I'll admit that. You didn't play the sort of hockey you can play, I'll tell you that. Because you've had a fine cause of the SCJs ever since you got into the series."

"What are the SCJs?"

"Stanley Cup Jitters, my boy. That's what you've got. And you'd better shake 'em off or the Porter family is going to find itself behind the eight ball."

"You mean I've got stage fright?"

"Stage fright or ice fright or whatever you want to call it. I've seen a veteran of twelve seasons in the NHL come down with it and make an unholy show of himself. Pressure. You think the whole weight of the hockey world is on your shoulders and it's too much for you."

Bud knew Amby Porter had put his finger directly on the trouble. The responsibility, the terrific strain of knowing that one little mistake might cost his team a goal, which might cost them a game, which might cost them a world championship—that was what had been getting him down.

"What's the cure?" he asked his father.

"Stop reading the papers, for one thing," bellowed Amby Porter suddenly. He snatched up the offending sheet from the table and hurled it into a corner.

"The way the sports writers go to town on the Stanley Cup series or a World Series in baseball, or a heavyweight championship prize fight—dramatizing them, colouring them up—it's enough to make anyone lose his sense of proportion."

"Yes, but—"

"Stop reading the papers. Don't listen to one solitary sports commentator on the radio until this is over. Don't listen to a hockey fan. Don't talk hockey at all. Don't even think it. Have you heard much hockey talked in the dressing room these nights?"

"Not much."

"Why not? Because smart players know it would only increase the pressure. And when you get out there in the next game—"

"You're going to use me?"

"I figure my judgment of hockey players is still pretty good, no matter how many sports writers think they could do better. You're in there until you prove me wrong."

Amby Porter got up and strode out of the room. Bud stared at his plate. For all his father's contempt for the sports writers, Bud knew there was plenty of truth in what he had just read. And the most uncomfortable truth of all was in the last line. As the series went, so went Amby Porter's chances for a renewal of his contract as manager of the Blues.

• • •

THE BLUES went into the sixth game fighting mad. They snagged a goal for themselves in the first five minutes of play, to the delirious joy of a hockey-wild crowd, and then settled down to the grim business of protecting their slim lead, with the hope of extending it on breakaways.

"Backcheck!" growled Amby Porter at his men. "Backcheck and keep right on backchecking. Wear 'em down!"

The Blues did just that. They made their opponents carry the play to them. Once in a while they would get a break, and a forward would go racing down the ice on a lone foray, but the Reds were fast and cagy. They got back swiftly, and their goalie, after that first tally, settled down to the job of being unbeatable.

"Remember what I told you," Amby Porter said to his son the first time he sent Bud out. "Keep your head up and do your best. If we win, you won't deserve the credit, and if we lose, you won't deserve the blame."

Bud tried to forget that he was playing for the championship of the world. He went out and backchecked.

Renault, who had a mean tongue and a deceptive way of dealing out the butt end of a stick during skirmishes along the boards, gave him the works, tried to peeve him into retaliation and penalties. Bud took it and stuck to business, which was to keep Renault handcuffed and plug up that side lane. They struggled through the second period, hanging on to that one-goal lead. They went into the third and the Reds opened up more and more.

They came into the stretch, down into the last ten minutes, the last five, the last three. Amby Porter sat up a little straighter on the bench. His face was like rock. He was quivering with suspense but his expression didn't show it. There was an offside at the Blues' line.

"All right, fellows," said Amby Porter huskily, as he sent out reserves. "Hold 'em."

Bud, rested after six minutes on the bench, swooped over to his spot on the wing. For the first time that night, he was quaking. Three minutes away from tying up the series again. The Reds would shoot the works. Hold them out for three minutes. Three minutes!

The Blues faltered. Their goalie had to make half a dozen quick saves. Bud, hanging on to Renault, saw that the defence was crumbling. The puck went flying into a corner and he chased Renault after it. Renault tried to hoist him into the boards, but he dodged and collared the puck. Renault crowded him, hacking at his stick. Bud heard a stick rap sharply on the ice, just a few feet away. Harried by Renault, he threw a blind pass. Then he looked up. Bradley, the Red centre, had the disk on the end of his stick, in the clear and right on the doorstep. Bradley took one stride and fired. The puck plunked into the rigging.

Bud Porter had fallen for the oldest gag in hockey—the faked pass signal—and the Reds had tied the score. The resentful roar of the crowd came rumbling down from the farthest rows. Aghast, Bud stood staring at the Blue goalie, who was sprawled on the ice and gazing up at him with the incredulous expression of one who has been double-crossed by his best friend.

A substitute came tumbling from the players' bench and nodded to him. Amby Porter didn't use his son again that night. He didn't dare. Bud had gone to pieces. The Blues squeezed out their win finally, but it took eighteen minutes of overtime before they got the extra goal.

Costly because Heffernan, their second-string centre, was carried off the ice with a skate gash in his leg, and Ross, the goalie, got struck in the face during a pileup and played the last five minutes with one eye tightly shut.

The Blues had won, the series would go to the limit, but Amby Porter was fuming when the team straggled back into the dressing room.

"Now will you learn to look up when you lay down a

pass?" he bellowed at Bud. "Here we go into a final game away from home with two men hurt, just because you got the jitters again. No thanks to you that we didn't lose tonight!"

Bud had no comeback. There was no doubt about it this time. He had flopped, and flopped so badly that if the Blues didn't take the Cup, their failure could be pinned on him alone.

"Guess you won't want me to make the trip," said Bud to his father.

"Did I say so?"

"No, but—"

"Until you hear otherwise, then, you're still with this team," grunted Amby Porter.

• • •

NEWSPAPERMEN were now crowding into the dressing room. They surrounded Amby Porter. "What have you got to say, Amby?" one of them asked.

The old-timer shrugged. "Usual stuff, boys. It was a tough game, but we won on our merits, and now that the chips are down, I'm confident my boys are good enough to take 'em on their own ice."

"But you didn't have much luck on the road during the regular playing schedule," objected one. "They only dropped one game to you on their own ice during the season."

"That was regular-season hockey," said Amby brusquely. "This is something else again—Stanley Cup hockey. I admit our road record hasn't been so hot. Forget it."

"Planning any changes?"

"I've got to bring up a boy from the farm team to replace Heffernan. Have to juggle my lines a little. Losing him is a tough break."

One of the sports writers looked Amby in the eye. "Using Bud in the final game?"

Amby gave him the look right back. "Why not?"

"We got a statement from one of the club directors. He says he thinks you're playing favourites. Says the kid played a terrible game and that, if you lose the series, he'll never vote to renew your contract next year."

"That's one man's opinion," snapped Amby Porter. "But I'm still managing this team and if I use Bud in Thursday night's game, it will be because I think he can play the Stanley Cup brand of hockey, not because he's my kid. He made a bad pass tonight. So what? Did you see any other bad passes made during that game?"

"Half a dozen. But they didn't cost goals."

"It was just Bud's tough luck that his bad pass did cost a goal. But let me say this: the Reds are a swell team. On tonight's play, they deserved at least one goal. A shut out wouldn't have given the true measure of that outfit, and you can quote me as saying that, as my tribute to a great hockey team."

Thus deftly did Amby Porter handle the press. Bud and everyone else in the room knew it was the old malarkey, but the quote would read well and remove some of the curse from Bud's mistake.

• • •

THE SERIES would end where it began: the Blues holed up in a private hotel off the beaten path and the next day was spent in rest and slumber. Some played cards; they visited each other's rooms; some read the newspapers. Bud Porter didn't. He had a pretty good idea what the newspaper accounts of his performance would be like. That evening, his father took him out to a movie with two other younger members of the team. Hockey wasn't mentioned.

Amby Porter knew something about pre-game pressure. Some high-strung players could worry themselves into a state of collapse before they ever stepped on the ice, and then suddenly became cool and iron-nerved. Others, outwardly calm, might come down with a violent case of the jitters the moment they left the bench. In Bud's case, it broke out under actual playing pressure, in the stress of the game itself.

"All I can do," Amby Porter told himself, "is to try to keep the kid's mind relaxed, and trust luck that he'll snap out of it."

But when he came into the dressing room the next evening and took a glance at Bud, his heart sank. Bud's mouth was tense and drawn; there were little telltale signs of nerves strung to the snapping point.

"How do you feel, boy?" asked Amby quietly.

"Fine."

"That's good. I just had a talk with Pennell."

Pennell was the club president.

Bud looked up quickly. "About your contract?"

Amby Porter grinned. He slapped Bud's knee. "Everything's going to be all right, no matter how this game comes out."

That took a weight off Bud's mind. The Blues might lose the Cup, but at least his father wouldn't lose his job on that account. Bud felt so lighthearted when he was sent out at the six-minute mark that he found himself playing without strain, playing cool, heads-up hockey, as if this was no different from a hundred other games.

The Reds nicked the first goal at seventeen minutes, but the Blues countered thirty seconds later when their first-stringers waltzed through with a swift triple-passing play that they cashed for the equalizer. The teams went into the second period on even terms.

• • •

THE GAME GOT ROUGH. Midway through the second period, the players began to crack under the pressure of hard going and a tied score in a tied series. Sticks were carried high. It exploded in a grand free-for-all down behind the Red net when the Red goalie tripped a forward streaking past the net.

Bud stayed out of it as the referee sorted out the combatants and began dealing out penalties. He leaned up against the boards, close to the back screen.

"I wouldn't like to be in Amby Porter's shoes right now," he heard a man in a rinkside seat saying. "This game is too close for comfort."

"Oh, I guess he can take it if the team loses," returned the man in the next seat.

"I was talking to a friend of mine in the press box between periods. He says Pennell told Amby Porter that it was win or else—"

"Else what?"

"Else the Blues have a new manager next year. That's official."

Bud stiffened. *Everything's going to be all right, no matter how this game comes out.*

That was what Amby Porter had said, but it didn't mean what Bud thought it meant. All it meant was that Amby Porter was trying to put him easy in his mind, trying to ease the strain and pressure. Bud was as taut as a fiddle-string when the teams squared away again, the Blues with a man in the penalty box, but the Reds two players short.

Struggling with Renault behind the blue line a few moments later, he wrenched himself clear just in time to see the puck come skipping across the ice, right to his stick. Bud slashed at it frantically, sent it skimming and bouncing far down the ice. He felt sick when he looked up and saw that the Blues didn't have a man back. He had been in the clear for a breakaway and a clear road to the goal and didn't know it. Renault went racing back for the puck, which had come to rest against the end boards.

Bud caught his father's eye. Amby Porter made a curt gesture. Bud skated to the gate as a substitute scrambled out to take his place.

Amby Porter never gave pep talks. In the rest session

between periods he simply said:

"Fellows, you've had a long season. You look pretty tired and banged up. You've played good hockey all through and tonight you've played swell hockey. You're going to win, because you're the best team. So get this last twenty minutes over with, and then we'll forget about hockey until next fall."

Bud had no hope that he would be used in the last period at all. But promptly at the six-minute mark when lines were changed, Amby Porter sent him out as usual.

The score was still tied. Bud would have been willing to trade in five years of his life for that extra goal, and he went after it like a madman. Anything to show the world that Amby Porter had been right.

Bud snatched up a pass at mid-ice, shook off Renault, tore across the blue line, and tried to crash the defence single-handed. The result was that he got tossed on his ear, and the Reds broke away on a rush that almost sent the red light flickering.

Bud skated back like mad. There was only a single thought in his mind—to get that goal if he had to skate himself into exhaustion doing it. He charged in again, saw a defenceman loom up ahead just as the loose puck rolled out. He lunged for it and pushed the rubber into a wild pileup of players just outside the crease. And then the defenceman hit him.

Bud had a clear glimpse of the goal light gleaming red behind the back screen as he pitched head foremost against the goal post. Then there was a violent, stunning shock, and blackness.

"The crazy kid!" howled Amby Porter. "He'll be lucky if he didn't break his neck." And then Amby let up a louder howl than ever. For the referee was shaking his head; the goalie had the puck wedged tightly between skate and post, right on the line. The score was still tied.

Bud opened his eyes and blinked in the dressing room light. Jimmy Hales, the trainer, was sponging his face. Bud sat up, groggily, gave his head a shake, and slipped unsteadily down from the rubbing table.

"I've gotta get out there, Jimmy," he mumbled. "They're still playing aren't they?"

"Five minutes to go," grunted Jimmy Hales. "You got a bump on your head as big as an egg. Better stay here."

"Stay here while the game is still on?" yelled Bud. "Where's my stick?"

The trainer was happy to see him leave. He wanted to see that last five minutes himself, even if the Blues were two goals down by now. And although he knew Bud would have a rousing headache before long, his skull was still in one piece.

Bud cast a hurried glance at the clock and smiled. He reached the bench and sat down beside Amby Porter.

"Five minutes. And we're two goals up!" he gloated, seeing the big "3" and "1" above and beneath the clock. "We're in, Dad!"

Amby Porter's mouth opened. He was just about to growl, "You're readin' those figures wrong, son," when he decided to hold his tongue. "Go out on the next change," he said.

Thirty seconds later, at the next offside, Bud was off the bench before the referee's whistle had stopped blowing. Three to one, he was thinking. Two goals up. The Reds would never make that up—not even if they shot the goalie. Amby Porter's job was safe for another year. That cloud wasn't hanging over his head anymore. Of course, if there was a chance to grab another goal just for good measure—

The chance came. It came before he had been out there two minutes. A long forward pass that he reached just at the blue line, a pass back to centre, a wide shot. Bud went in after the rebound. Not in a wild frenzy, as if the fate of nations depended on it, but swiftly, neatly, hooking it away from a defenceman who tried to give him the hip. After all, they were two goals up.

Bud took his time, flipped the puck over. Harris, at full momentum, picked it up and let fly. A masked shot, with his own centre ahead of him. A backhander that no goalie could have blocked. The puck whipped into the twine. And this time, when the red light shone, the referee didn't shake his head.

The Reds, seeing their lead whittled down to one lone goal, were shaken. They packed their defence, which puzzled Bud Porter mightily. It should be the other way around, but he didn't have much time to think about it in the wild struggle that ensued at the red line. Coolly, he picked up a pass and blistered a shot that just skimmed outside the post. A Red defenceman charged him, stick high, and he went into the boards with a crash. The whistle shrilled. The defenceman was thumbed to the penalty box.

Bud picked himself up, groggy all over again, and a substitute tapped him. "I'm takin' over, Bud."

Bud skated to the bench. He managed a grin as he came in.

"Three goals up and three minutes to go, Dad," he chirped. "They won't catch us now."

"Three goals up, my neck!" bawled Amby Porter, leaping

up and down in his excitement. "We're within a goal of tying the score, and we've got the odd man! We've got a chance now! A chance!"

Bud sagged. He flopped to the bench. He stared at the clock again and blinked. Just as in the home rink—visitors' score in the lower slot, home team score in the upper. But the Blues were the visitors this time.

Then the jitters swept all over him again, as he watched his teammates pitch into the faltering, short-handed Reds. They were swept away in a wild rush of insane delight when the power play cracked the Red defence, and a Blue forward tricked his way into the clear, picked up a short pass and banged it home over a prostrate goalie.

A two-goal lead wiped out in as many minutes, and a man in the penalty box. The tiring Reds broke. They broke wide open. Even the return of their penalized player didn't save them. The Blues were climbing, the Reds were on the way out.

At nineteen minutes, the Blue centre swooped around the back of the net and hooked the puck around the goal post for the tie breaker.

• • •

AMBY PORTER tossed his son a folded newspaper at break-fast on the train next morning. "Read that, boy." he said with a grin.

Bud didn't read more than a few lines.

Undoubtedly the turning point of the game was Bud Porter's surprise assist that put the Blues back into the fight when they seemed thoroughly beaten. Porter, whose inexperience had made him the weak link of the outfit earlier in the series, redeemed himself by the prettiest play of the night when he picked his way out of a corner and laid down a perfect pass to Harris, who whipped in the goal that sent the Blues on their way—

Bud reached for the coffee. "Yeah, I'm a swell player," he said. "Just give me a two-goal lead and I ain't afraid of anybody."

"Just let anybody try to tell me I can't pick hockey players," beamed Amby Porter. "Now that you've got those Stanley Cup Jitters out of your system—boy, next season we'll show 'em!"

THE SOFTY AT CENTRE ICE

THERE WAS A CHEER from the railbirds watching the practice session of the Riverglen Lions, as Thompson, the first-string centre, drew a defenceman out of position with a fake pass, then bolted through the gap with the puck and stormed in on the goal. He held his shot, made the goalie come out to him, then beat the net tender cleanly with his drive into the twine.

Haines, the coach, a sturdy, grizzled hockey veteran from way back, nodded in approval and looked at his watch.

"OK!" he called out to the players. "Three times around the rink and you're through!"

Thompson skated swiftly up the boards. The other players fell into line behind him. In silence, they sped around the rink, once, twice, three times, and then came skidding and scraping to a stop at the gate. They clumped off to the dressing room.

John P. Taylor, manager of the foundry and president of the hockey club, was sitting in the players' box. He had come out that evening to watch the squad in action, for the schedule was due to open in less than a week, and he wanted to see how the new coach and the new team were shaping up.

"What do you think, Mr. Taylor?" asked Haines.

This job in Riverglen meant a lot to Haines, a one-time professional star, who made his living by coaching hockey teams in the wintertime and running a boys' camp in the summer. But in hockey, as in everything else, all the world loves a winner and nothing succeeds like success.

Five years had passed since Haines had managed a winning team. For a while, it had looked as if he mightn't get a berth this winter at all, because a coach's reputation depends on his ability to bring home winners. The boys' camp hadn't been doing so well, either. Haines had a pretty fair idea that Riverglen was his last chance.

"Fine!" said Taylor, beaming. "You've done wonders with them. You have a team there."

"Good material to work with."

"They should be good. Heaven knows we had enough trouble rounding them up."

Haines knew all about that. He knew perfectly well that Riverglen was not a hometown outfit. It was an old story. Amateur hockey competition was so keen that there just wasn't any such animal as a hometown team among the top-flight squads any more.

"At that," said Taylor, "we're still amateur."

He said it with pride. Everyone knew that many of the first-rank amateur outfits were amateur in name only; that their packed teams represented formidable payrolls.

"They'll do," agreed Haines.

"We were lucky to get the men we've got," returned Taylor. "It's easy enough to get players if you want to put some cash money on the line, but Mrs. Dudley won't stand for it. Jobs, yes. Salaries, no. By the way, she said she wanted to see you tonight. You're to go up to the house."

Haines nodded. Mrs. Dudley, widow of the man who had founded the stove and furnace works, was the real owner of the hockey team. In fact, as head of the town's only industry, she just about controlled everything in Riverglen, including the rink.

"I'll go up right away," he said.

• • •

MRS. DUDLEY was a pleasant, old-fashioned little woman, and she lived in a pleasant, old-fashioned little house on the hill that overlooked the town. Wealthy though she was, Mrs. Dudley still lived as simply and modestly as in the days when her late husband was struggling to get the foundry under way. A motherly dumpling of a woman, she had a heart as big as a pumpkin and knew every man, woman, child, dog, and cat in Riverglen by their first names.

She was not alone when she received Haines in the parlour. With her was a slim, shy, good-looking youth so exquisitely attired that Haines felt like the milkman by comparison. Fair hair plastered sleekly to his skull, a small moustache, a powder-blue suit nicely tailored, and pearl-gray spats over gleaming shoes.

"I'm so glad you called, Mr. Haines," said Mrs. Dudley, smiling at him happily. "I want you to meet my nephew, Clarence."

"The name *would* be Clarence," Haines said to himself, regarding this lily of the field with disfavour; but he was surprised at the energy of the young man's grip when they shook hands.

"Pleasure, sir," murmured Clarence, politely but shyly.

"Clarence has been living with my sister in Boston for the past few years," Mrs. Dudley explained. "Now that he is through school, I have persuaded him to come and spend the winter in Riverglen."

Haines was wondering what all this had to do with him. To his horror, he soon found out.

"Clarence," said Mrs. Dudley, "is very fond of hockey. Agatha—that's my sister—tells me he is very good at it. He took skating lessons from one of the best professionals in the country. I have asked Clarence if he wouldn't play for our little team here in Riverglen, and he says he will. Isn't that nice?"

Haines almost groaned aloud. But he knew very well that Mrs. Dudley's word was law in Riverglen. If her nephew wished to play hockey, her nephew would play hockey, be he ever so terrible.

"That will be fine," he gulped. "What position do you play?" he asked Clarence.

"Any of them, except goal," answered Clarence in his cultured voice. "I prefer playing at centre ice, however."

"It's so fortunate," gurgled Mrs. Dudley, "that we have a team here so Clarence will be able to play his favourite game." She beamed fondly at Clarence over the top of her spectacles. "But you must see that the other boys aren't too rough, Mr. Haines. Clarence has never been very strong. He had a nervous breakdown when he was twelve."

"You mustn't worry about me, aunt, really," said Clarence, smoothing his hair. "If it's quite all right with you, old man," he told Haines, "I'll be glad to turn out to practice any time you say."

Haines felt ill. Naturally, he couldn't afford to argue with Clarence's aunt. She could shut down all hockey in Riverglen at a moment's notice if she took it into her head to do so. But what sort of hockey team was he going to have with the elegant Clarence at centre ice? He had spent weeks whipping his outfit into shape, and now that they were ready to go, every man playing his position to the king's taste, along came this bespatted Bostonian to heave a monkey wrench into the works.

"Tomorrow night," gulped Haines unhappily. "Glad to have you."

"Tomorrow night, sir?" said Clarence. "Right. Shall we say—ah—seven o'clock?"

"We shall," Haines muttered. "Er—I mean, yes. Practice is at seven."

"Righto!" Clarence assured him brightly. "I'll be there on the dot."

Haines left the house in a daze. He was talking to himself as he made his way back downtown.

• • •

THERE WAS PRETTY nearly a riot in the dressing room next evening when Haines broke the news to his team that he was shifting his second forward line around to make room for young Mr. Dudley at centre.

"What?" howled Sandy Oliver, who had been slated for that centre berth ever since John P. Taylor had written to him the previous summer offering him a good job in the foundry on the strength of his reputation as a promising hockey player. "Shift me to the wing? Nothing doing. You can't pull a stunt like that on me."

"I'm sorry. You'll have to go on the wing."

"And how about me?" yelped Hack Riddell, already holding down the right-wing spot on the second line.

"We'll just have to use you as a sort of utility forward, I guess," said Haines. "It's tough luck, Hack, but I can't fix it up any other way."

"Utility forward! I know what that means. I don't get into uniform at all unless somebody gets sick or breaks a leg. I've got to give up my position to Sandy, and he has to give up his position to this new guy—nix!" He threw his gloves on the floor. So did Oliver.

"I won't stand for it," declared Oliver. "I play centre or not at all."

Haines knew how to handle mutiny. "OK. Turn in your

uniform," he said crisply. "Dudley is playing, whether you like it or not."

Oliver couldn't get a transfer to any other amateur team that winter, and he knew it. After a few rebellious mutterings he began to climb into his gear. Riddell, however, started for the door.

"Walk out that door," said Haines indifferently, "and you needn't bother to come back."

Riddell hesitated. "Holy cats!" he exploded in disgust. "I came here to play hockey, not to hang around as a blamed utility man."

"I'm doing the best I can, Hack. Stick around. Maybe you'll get more hockey than you expect."

At that moment, the door opened and Clarence Dudley oozed meekly into the dressing room. He wore a derby hat, a gorgeous silk scarf, and yellow gloves.

"Good evening, chaps!" said Clarence.

Eyes travelled coldly from the spats to the derby hat. A few surly grunts acknowledged Clarence's cheery salutation. He was an interloper, an outsider who had made the team by his drag rather than by merit. The Lions wanted no part of him.

Haines introduced Clarence around in a perfect fog of disapproval. But frigid reception didn't seem to bother

Clarence, however, and when he was shown his locker he began getting into uniform with vim.

"I expect I'll be a little crude at first, old man," he told Haines. "The hockey we played at school may have been a bit different. I'll be very grateful for any little suggestions."

Cassidy and Leblanc, the big defencemen, winked at each other and began whispering in a corner. They were cooking up something, Haines knew.

Clarence stripped well. He was light but wiry. Haines told himself that if Clarence would only shave off that fool moustache and wash the grease out of his hair he would look all right.

Haines had enough regulars and spares for two teams and now he lined up his first-string forwards in front of a sub-defence and the sub-goalie. Clarence, with the wrathful Oliver and a winger named Pelletier, made up the other line ahead of Cassidy and Leblanc, with Henderson in the cage.

Thompson and Clarence faced off.

"Go to it, boys," said Haines, and dropped the puck. He noticed Mrs. Dudley, beaming proudly, sitting beside John P. Taylor among the handful of railbirds.

Thompson and Lodge, first-string forwards, Oliver and Riddell, and big Cassidy were the five players who had been imported to bolster up the Riverglen team that year. Pelletier and Clark had been recruited from the previous year's juniors. Leblanc, Henderson, and the other two defence men were old-timers with Riverglen.

It did not take Haines more than a few minutes to find out that Clarence could skate. He was fast as a streak on the steel blades and he knew how to handle a stick. But when it came to playing that centre-ice position, he couldn't seem to get anywhere.

Thompson led a rush on goal and lost the puck at the defence. Oliver went around the net with the disk and came back up his wing. The opposing forwards skated back, as Clarence and Pelletier fell in line with Oliver for the rush. Oliver passed just as he met his check. The puck skimmed over to Clarence, but it wasn't laid onto his stick. It was about six inches behind him, and he had to reach back for it. By that time, Thompson was on top of him, stole the puck neatly, and broke away.

A little later, it happened again. Pelletier sent over a pass to centre. This time, it was too far ahead, and Clarence fumbled it. Shortly afterward, on another rush, Clarence flipped a pass to Oliver, and this, too, went astray.

Haines looked grim. He knew perfectly well what was happening.

"So the boys have decided to give him the works, eh?"

He let it go for a while, but the new forward line wasn't even getting into the defence zone. Clarence's wings simply wouldn't play with him. Haines groaned and told Thompson and Clarence to switch places.

The situation was no better. Lodge and Clark fell into the spirit of the thing. When Clarence passed, the puck invariably went wide of the mark. If he was waiting for a pass, the puck invariably came to him at such a bad angle that he muffed it. His wings jockeyed him offside when he tried to lead an attack.

Haines skated up beside Lodge. "Lay off that stuff," he snapped, "or I'll send you in." He told Clark the same thing.

"Why start riding me?" demanded Clark. "Can I help it if the dope can't take a pass?"

But the pair stopped fooling and began giving Clarence a few passes he could handle. Clarence snapped up one of these, stepped around Thompson, and broke for the defence. He came in fast on Cassidy's side, swung out, and zipped the puck across to Clark. And Cassidy stepped into him.

For a practice session Cassidy displayed extraordinary enthusiasm as he let Clarence have hip, shoulder, stick, knee and everything in the book. The fair-haired nephew of

Mrs. Dudley bounced about three feet and went sprawling on the ice as if he had been smacked by a truck.

Haines didn't say anything. The check was illegal, and in a game it would have earned Cassidy a jaunt to the penalty box. But Haines wanted to see how Clarence would take it.

Groggily, the newcomer got to his feet. "Sorry!" he gasped and limped away.

Cassidy and his defencemate gaped at each other.

"Did you hear that?" grunted Cassidy. "I smear him all over the ice and he says he's sorry."

Clarence went back to his position. The opposing forwards began bumping him. Oliver sloughed him into the boards and dumped him with a crash that could be heard the length of the rink. Haines waited to see if Clarence would toss his gloves to the ice and pile into the wingman. Surely Clarence would realize by now that they were giving him a sleigh ride, and that his only chance of making them respect him was to mop up the ice with at least one of his tormentors.

Up he got. "Sorry!" he remarked, shaking his head.

"Yellow, too, huh?" taunted Oliver, who was spoiling for a fight.

Clarence merely skated away, smiling vaguely as if he hadn't heard.

They were tough, hard-boiled players, jealous of their positions, and they were out to run Clarence off the team if they could, for the simple reason that they didn't think he was good enough to step with them.

Haines decided to let it ride. "He'll either fight back or they'll make him so sick of this team that he'll be glad to hang up his skates," he told himself. "I'm hanged if I'll interfere."

To him, it looked like the best way of getting rid of Clarence.

After half an hour of it, Clarence's forward line had not scored a goal; they had worked in on the net for less than half a dozen shots; they had seen five goals scored against them, and Clarence had absorbed enough bumps to last the average hockey player through a hard winter. Not once had he complained to Haines; but, on the other hand, not once had he dished out a bodycheck on his own account.

"Why don't you sock some of those birds back again?" demanded Haines.

Clarence looked at him in surprise.

"I'll admit they're a little rougher than I've been accustomed to," he said. "But really, old man, would it be quite the thing to do? Our coach at school always stressed the science of the sport."

"I'd love to meet that coach," remarked Haines. "Did he ever play hockey?"

"Oh, no," replied Clarence. "He was the mathematics master. But he had studied a book about the game. Used to work out his own plays on the blackboard, y' know—all theory."

"Theories are all right, but a butt end in the belly is a fact," grunted Haines. "If I was you, I'd forget some of the theories and lay into these babies."

At the end of the workout, Clarence had a split lip, a discoloured eye, and a fine collection of bruises and contusions. But, after he had donned his spats and his derby again, he thanked Haines very politely.

"So long, you chaps. I'll be seeing you tomorrow," he said to his sour-faced teammates and disappeared.

• • •

THE RIVERGLEN BAND was playing, and the rink was packed. Nearly everyone in town was on hand for the opening game of the season. As the players grouped around the referee for instructions, Haines crouched moodily in the box with his chin on his chest.

They were opening the season against the Lawrence

Nighthawks, old rivals of the Lions, and the Nighthawks were definitely gunning for the amateur title this year. At that, Haines would have been content with his own team's chances had it not been for the second line of forwards. The line simply would not do. He had coaxed, cajoled, and threatened, but it had all been useless. The Lions resented Clarence. Haines knew most of the Nighthawks by reputation; knew that they were fast and experienced. In the first five minutes of the game, they showed it.

Then came the moment Haines dreaded. He had to relieve his starting line and send in Clarence Dudley, flanked by Oliver and Pelletier, to face the Lion second-stringers. Perhaps, hoped Haines, under actual playing conditions, the grievance against Clarence might be forgotten. But on the very first rush, when the three forwards worked their way through, and Oliver carried the puck in, the wingman wouldn't lay down a pass when Clarence was in the clear with a perfect opening. Instead, Oliver tried to play it on his own and lost the puck to a Nighthawk defenceman.

It didn't take the Nighthawks long to find out that this second line wasn't clicking. They began pressing harder, turned on the heat, launched rush after rush. Wilkes, the Nighthawk centre on the second line, gave Clarence a bad roughing against the boards, and as Clarence came out of it Haines heard him gasp, "Sorry, old man!"

"Ow!" groaned Haines.

A little later, Wilkes handed Clarence a solid bodycheck, knocked him flat and sailed through for a solo goal.

"And that's that!" muttered Haines disconsolately, as he yanked the line and sent out his first-stringers.

"Can't we even get our breath?" demanded Thompson as they went out. The forwards were accustomed to a longer rest than Haines had granted them. They knew why the coach was sending them out so quickly. The second line wasn't standing up. Naturally, they blamed Clarence. More ill feeling!

Disgruntled, the first-string forwards laid into the Nighthawks and got the goal back on a neat short-passing attack that left the goalie sprawled helpless on the ice while Lodge walked in on the open cage for a soft counter. But Haines couldn't leave that line out there for the whole period. He left them on the ice as long as he dared, then sent out his Clarence string again.

This time, the Nighthawks pitched in fiercely, fed passes to their centre, and concentrated their attack on Clarence as the weak spot of the line. They began bumping him hard. Clarence never retaliated, took it all, didn't attempt so much as a bodycheck in return. And with his wings giving him pathetic support, he had little chance. Two quick goals resulted.

Haines was mighty glum when the period ended. It wasn't that Oliver and Pelletier were actually laying down on the job. They simply lacked all confidence in their centre and refused to take chances on him.

Haines couldn't blame them entirely.

There was silence in the dressing room during the rest period. Haines didn't have anything to say. They were in for a licking, and they would just have to take it. He couldn't beat the Nighthawks with one forward line at cross purposes.

"Well, come on," growled Oliver sourly when the three-minute bell sounded. "May as well go out there and get it over with."

Clarence hadn't said a word. All through the rest period he had sat humped over on the bench, staring at the floor. He glanced over at Oliver now, opened his mouth as if to speak, then evidently changed his mind. He shook his head a little and began tightening up his laces.

Haines used his first-stringers as much as he dared in that second period. They worked hard, played brilliant hockey, even outplayed the Nighthawks, and punched in another goal in the first ten minutes. But they couldn't stand the pace without relief.

The visitors were wise to the situation by now. Again they laced into Clarence, checked him to a standstill, and concentrated all their attacks on centre. Oliver and Pelletier made frantic efforts to stem the tide, but they were out of luck. The Lions were swept back, disorganized. The Nighthawks rammed in two more goals in as many minutes.

The Riverglen crowd was steeped in gloom. Their team was taking a licking—a bad one. And as the period went on, the Lions got worse and the Nighthawks better.

"This," reflected Haines bitterly, "just about means my finish as a hockey coach."

The score was 6–2 at the end of the second period, and the third was a runaway affair. Three more goals were scored against the Clarence line and another against the first-stringers. By that time the crestfallen fans were beginning to file out of the rink. As a season's opener, it was probably the worst debacle in the history of Riverglen hockey. The crowd was bewildered. On paper, it simply couldn't happen. Riverglen had imported players every bit as good as the Nighthawk stars. Haines knew he was up against it. A few more games like that and the Riverglen team would simply fold up and let the rest of the schedule go by default.

In the dressing room, the players dressed sullenly and hurried out. Haines didn't have anything to say to them. What was the use? They knew the trouble as well as he did. He noticed that Clarence took a long time about getting out of his gear, and was slow and deliberate getting into his street clothes. Finally, he was alone with the coach. Clarence, knotting his necktie with care, remarked, "I say, Mr. Haines, I hope you don't mind, but I imagine you had better get some one else for that centre-ice position. I don't think I care to go on with it."

Haines looked up, startled. Clarence quitting! He had expected anything but that. But new hope surged up in him. Without Clarence, he might be able to get somewhere with this team.

"What's the trouble?" he said.

"As a matter of fact," observed Clarence, "the hockey here is a bit rougher than I've been accustomed to." He smoothed down his hair, donned his overcoat, adjusted his scarf with care, and put his hat on at an exact angle. He did not look at Haines. "You'll be able to get along without me, I imagine."

Then he turned and extended his hand to the coach. "Many thanks for your kindness, sir. I appreciate it very much."

"Why—why, that's all right, lad. I'm sorry you feel you'd better drop out—"

But while Haines was still floundering, Clarence swung his skates over his shoulder and sauntered out, whistling softly.

In spite of his heartfelt relief, Haines was a little sorry to see Clarence go. He had a notion that Clarence wasn't quitting because the going was tough. Clarence was quitting for the good of the team.

• • •

HAINES FELT a lot better when he watched his squad in action at the next practice. With Oliver back at centre, and Riddell and Pelletier flanking him, the second line clicked smartly.

With Clarence gone, the morale of the team improved. They were anxious to wipe out the disgrace of that opening-game massacre. The opportunity came when the schedule sent them out of town at the end of the week to tangle with the Carfax Bulldogs.

The Carfax squad, like the Nighthawks, was hand-picked. The Carfax hockey executive had gone on the principle that one must fight fire with fire and that there was no use trying to stay in that league with a hometown team.

The game with the Bulldogs was a rough and stormy session, but the Lions came out of it covered with goals and glory. There were three fist fights, the penalty box was occupied most of the time, and the game was an old-time brawl. The Riverglen team didn't back down an inch, weathered the heavy bumping in fine style, and limped off the ice with a 4–1 victory.

It was a four-team league, and the Lions' next engagement was a home game against the Newcastle Sailors, weak opponents of the loop. The Sailors had a first-rate starting line, but had a weak sub-list. The Lions took the game by a 7–3 count with their second line accounting for four goals.

The Riverglen fans took the team to their hearts again and cheered mightily.

The real test came when the Lions went to Lawrence for their return clash with the Nighthawks. All the players were up on their toes, eager to avenge their previous defeat.

The Nighthawks were a hard team to beat on their own ice at any time; and after the cricket score of the opening game, the Lions weren't conceded a chance. However, they provided one of the most rousing struggles that had been seen in the league in many a moon and battled their way to a 2–2 overtime tie.

Haines hadn't seen anything of Clarence since the night the lad turned in his uniform. For several days, he had expected to be called on the carpet by Mrs. Dudley. But evidently Clarence hadn't taken his woes to his aunt, and the next time Haines encountered that lady, she was surprisingly agreeable.

"I'm so glad you're having success with the hockey team, Mr. Haines," she said. "Clarence tells me you are a very good coach."

"Um—yes—Clarence—" stammered Haines.

"He told me he thought he wasn't quite good enough to play with the Lions," continued Mrs. Dudley. "He's really very modest, Mr. Haines, but I suppose he knows best. He went up to his uncle's farm for the rest of the winter."

Evidently Mrs. Dudley bore no ill will, and that put Haines in a better frame of mind.

• • •

AS THE SEASON went on, the Lions dropped a game to the Bulldogs, but redeemed themselves when they squeezed out a 3–2 win over the Nighthawks before a wild-eyed, exuberant Riverglen mob. Then the lowly Sailors astonished every one, including themselves, by knocking off the Bulldogs in a rip-roaring battle that nearly ended in a riot.

It became, in short, one of those series in which anything may happen, a neck-and-neck race to the wire with the hockey fans in a mounting frenzy of excitement. Every game drew a packed house. And as the schedule neared the end, it became plain that the issue lay between the Nighthawks and the Lions, with the Bulldogs trailing in third place.

What was generally regarded as the crucial game of the whole season, was the third clash of the Lions-Nighthawks series, played in Lawrence. The winning team would have a strangle hold on first place.

Haines was an anxious man as his team skated out to meet the Nighthawks that evening. But in his heart he knew that his team was good enough to turn the trick. The Nighthawks had not been slipping, either. They had dropped a couple of hard games to the Bulldogs, but they were now a smooth-working machine that looked good enough to give an argument to any team in the ranks of the amateurs. It was a fast, brilliant game, that third clash between the Lions and their old rivals. And when it was all over, Haines came back to Riverglen with a winning team, and a title within his grasp. The reception of the Lions at home was tumultuous. There was a big crowd at the station to meet the team.

"Good work!" beamed John P. Taylor, shaking Haines warmly by the hand. "It's in the bag."

Years in hockey, that most uncertain of all games, had shown Haines the folly of counting chickens before they are hatched.

"The Nighthawks still have an outside chance," he reminded Taylor.

"Outside is right," guffawed Taylor. "Why, it's just mathematical. They have to win their last game while you're losing your last two before they can even tie. It'll be all over as soon as you beat the Sailors next week. You haven't dropped a game to 'em all season."

On paper it looked as if the Lions were in.

A title for the Lions meant a lot to Haines—more than any of them knew. During the week, he had received a letter from an old major league sidekick, now interested in the managerial end of the game, who had hinted that he was watching the league series with interest and that "something might be arranged" for next winter if things went well.

It was at this time that, somehow, in the few days that intervened before the date with the Sailors, Haines had a premonition of trouble. He felt it in his bones. There were whisperings in the dressing room. A couple of times, he surprised groups of his players in earnest discussion that ceased abruptly when he entered the room.

There was to be a light workout on the evening before they were to leave town for the game with the Sailors. Haines was just finishing supper in the local restaurant when his waitress told him he was wanted on the phone. The caller was Henderson, his goalie.

"Listen, Mr. Haines, mebbe you'd better beat it down to the station right away before that evening train pulls out," blurted Henderson. "I didn't know what was going on, honest, or I'd have tipped you off."

"What's up?"

"One of the boys up at the boarding house just phoned me that Thompson and Lodge have checked out. There was talk about them gettin' an offer from a pro team a few days ago, but I—"

Henderson was left talking to thin air. Haines dropped the receiver as if it had turned red hot in his hand, snatched up his hat and coat, plunged out of the restaurant without taking time to close the door behind him.

• • •

LODGE AND THOMPSON, left-winger and centre respectively of the Lions' starting line, may have had plenty of backbone in a hockey game, but they had been too spineless to tell Haines, face to face, that they were deserting the team. The train was already in, the two players already in their seats, when the coach found them.

They looked up, startled, shamefaced and guilty, when they saw Haines in the aisle.

"Going for a little trip, boys?" he said.

Thompson glanced at his companion. Then he muttered: "We left a letter at the boarding house for you, coach. We're pulling out."

"For good?"

Thompson nodded.

"We got an offer from the Blackbirds. Their major league team took up a couple of their men and left them short. It's a good chance for us to break into pro hockey, and we can't afford to pass it up."

Haines looked down at them grimly. "I suppose you realize this is a pretty rotten trick you're playing on me."

They shifted uneasily.

"You wouldn't wait one more day—not even one more day to see it through!" said Haines incredulously. "I've had a few cheap tricks pulled on me in my time—"

"We couldn't wait another day," snapped Thompson. "We have to report within twenty-four hours, and that's all there is to it. I don't care whether you think it's a cheap trick or not. We're not passing up a pro chance for the sake of a punk job in a stove factory."

The locomotive bell was clanging; the train lurched into motion.

"You pair of four-flushers!" gritted Haines and swung away. He hurried back down the aisle and sprang to the platform.

By the time he reached the rink, he had cooled down a little and was ready to take a calmer view of the situation. He had lost two of his best forwards, and they had to be replaced at once. Even at that, he felt that his team ought to be good enough to take the Sailors—the weakest team in the league—into camp.

"And, by George, we'll win that game!" growled Haines to himself.

In the dressing room, his remaining players were apathetically climbing into their uniforms. They all knew about the desertions by now, and it was plain that they believed the Lions were washed up.

"Listen, fellows," said Haines, "a couple of four-flushers have crossed us up, wrecked one of our forward lines. They won't be with us tomorrow night. The second line will start instead. I'm going to borrow a couple of lads from the town junior team as subs. Remember, all we have to do to win that title is take tomorrow night's game. And we're gonna do it. Are you with me?"

There was a mild cheer, but it wasn't as hearty as Haines would have liked.

Henderson, the goalie, however, said: "Attaboy, chief! Just watch our smoke."

• • •

HAINES DIDN'T LET the grass grow under his feet. He got on the telephone and summoned the centre and left-winger of the junior squad to come and work out.

Those youngsters, excited and gratified, were down at the rink and hustling into uniform within twenty minutes. He could count on them to give everything they had. And for the next hour Haines worked with them so that they might fit in with Clark as a second-string forward line that might at least be passable.

Dayton, the junior centre, was a gawky, earnest lad with a nice turn of speed, but he was painfully lacking in experience, and he stood out like a sore thumb among the more finished senior puck chasers. Stewart, the new wing, was no better; but at least the pair tried hard and were wildly anxious to make good.

With Clark's experience to back them up, Haines figured that the line might backcheck efficiently enough to hold the fort while the first-stringers were resting up.

At last, he sent the squad to the dressing room. He had done the best he could. The rest lay in the laps of the hockey gods.

A crowd of Riverglen rooters accompanied the team on the trip to Carfax next day. Now, if ever, the Lions needed the support of their followers. Haines noticed that Oliver and Riddell sat together, engaged in earnest conversation during the entire journey, but he had no suspicion that anything was in the wind until half an hour before game time, when Oliver came to him.

"Hack and I have been talking things over," said the centre. "I think we ought to be able to knock these babies off tonight."

"I hope so."

"If we do, it'll give Riverglen the title. And no thanks to Thompson and Lodge, either. But Hack and I have been figuring we ought to get a little more out of this than just a job in the foundry."

Haines's mouth tightened. He knew what was coming now.

"For instance?"

"A little bonus if we win tonight's game."

"How much?"

"We figured that a couple of hundred bucks apiece would be fair."

"And if you don't get it?"

Oliver shrugged. "We think we should get it."

"Going to throw me down if you don't?"

Oliver didn't answer.

Haines played for time.

"I have no power to promise you the money. Wait until we get back to Riverglen."

"By that time, you'll have the title, and you'll tell us to go jump in the lake. You can telephone."

"A nice little holdup," said Haines evenly. "I'll let you know later."

He thought for a long time after Oliver left him. It would be easy enough to kid the two players along, promise them the money, and later deny any knowledge of it. After a while, he called John P. Taylor on long distance and told him the story.

"The blamed crooks!" exploded Taylor. "They've been

waiting for this chance all winter, I'll bet. What do you think we ought to do?"

"It's up to the hockey club, Mr. Taylor."

"I suppose we'll have to pay 'em. What's your advice?"

"If you pay them, the word will get around and the rest of the boys will expect something. It isn't fair to them."

It had been a hard decision to make, the most difficult decision of his whole hockey career. If the club didn't care to act on it, that was not his affair.

"By gosh," said Taylor, "I believe you're right. Stall 'em along if you can, but we won't pay them that money."

Oliver and Riddell weren't dumb. When Haines told them that the bonus matter would have to be discussed with John P. Taylor back in Riverglen next day, and that he had no power to promise them the money, they simply went out and turned in a listless performance in the first period against the Sailors.

The second-stringers worked hard, but their lack of experience was against them, and the best they could do was hold the Sailors off the score sheet.

"Listen, you two," gritted Haines between the periods. "If you don't get out there and play hockey next frame, I'll go to the amateur authorities and have you kicked clean out of the game."

"Where's your proof?" asked Oliver.

It would be his word against theirs. Haines knew they had him licked.

In the second period, Oliver and Riddell apparently tried hard. They checked industriously, broke up enemy attacks, but when they got within scoring range themselves, something always happened. Either a pass would go astray or a shot would miss the net, or it would be dead on the goalie's pads.

The Sailors, sensing that they were up against a weakened team, got down to business and got through Pelletier and the two juniors for a goal. Toward the end of the period, just to show what he could do if he cared, Oliver went through the whole Sailor team, pulled the goalie out—and then missed an open net.

"How about it, coach?" he asked in the rest period.

Haines knew that Riddell and Oliver could settle the whole issue in the final period if they felt like it. The temptation was strong.

"Nothing doing," he said shortly.

The Sailors got through for two more goals in the last period. In the dying moments of the game, Oliver and Riddell went through on a neat short-passing attack and rang up a counter that saved the Lions from a whitewashing. They had scored the only goal, and no goals had been scored against the team while they were on the ice. But the Lions had lost 3–1.

Haines, tight-lipped, faced them in the dressing room.

"Turn in your uniforms!" he snapped. "You two bandits are all washed up, so far as this team is concerned."

"Maybe the hockey club will think different," said Oliver. "We still have a game against the Nighthawks."

"Yeah, and we can beat 'em, too," Riddell said.

They were figuring that the hockey club would knuckle down and yield to their demands in the hope that the Lions might yet win the title by winning the game against the Nighthawks.

"I don't care if the Nighthawks beat us fifty to nothing," declared Haines. "You two are through. And if the club doesn't back me up in it, they can have my resignation."

The club did back him up. Oliver and Riddell were fired from the foundry next day, left for home the same night, and Haines was faced with the problem of meeting the Nighthawks minus four of his best forwards.

He had a strictly hometown, amateur team on his hands now. And who ever heard of an honest-to-goodness amateur outfit beating a squad like the Nighthawks?

John P. Taylor and some of the hockey club officials

hinted that it mightn't be a bad idea to let the game go by default. Haines wouldn't listen.

"Nothing doing!" he grunted. "If we're going to lose, we'll lose fighting."

• • •

HAINES DUG UP a couple of veteran players who hadn't donned a skate in five years, as well as two forwards who had tried out for the squad early in the season, but had failed to make the grade. Although he knew there was no chance of rebuilding his team now, the new material was even worse than he had expected.

"They're awful!" he groaned to John P. Taylor as he watched the recruits flounder through a nightmare work-out that evening.

"They're even worse than that," agreed Taylor. "It's going to be a shame to take money from the fans for the sort of exhibition they'll see when we hook up with the Nighthawks."

For a moment, Haines was tempted to agree with him, inclined to let the whole thing go by default. But that went against the grain; his nature rebelled against it.

"Even if the score is 10–1 against you, there's no excuse

for lying down," he said. "We'll play 'em."

Even the newcomers realized how punk they were. They came to Haines in a body after the workout and told him that if he could get any one else, they would be well content to watch the game from the sidelines.

"It ain't that we're afraid of the licking," said one, "but we figure that almost anybody out there would be able to play better than us."

"If I find anyone, I'll let you know," Haines assured him grimly.

He wouldn't find anyone. He knew that.

"The trouble with this business of importing hockey players from outside," he told Taylor, "is that you neglect the development of your own material. Now, if you had a juvenile league here, and then a town league to bring along the best of the material you develop in the juveniles, you'd have hockey players coming along all the time."

He paused and made a sweeping gesture with his hands.

"As it is, the Riverglen kids haven't any encouragement to learn the game. They figure they'll never have a chance to make the team against the star imports, anyway, so you're left high and dry in an emergency like this."

Taylor held up his hands. "Don't lecture me," he begged. "I'm off imports for life. Never again."

• • •

AT HALF PAST SEVEN on the night of the game with the Nighthawks, the coach went down to the rink. He was dispirited, but tried to conceal the fact. All his season's work had apparently toppled in ruins about him, and it looked as if his coaching career was at an end.

And then he gasped as he entered the dressing room. He blinked. There, on a bench, sat Clarence Dudley and three sheepish, red-faced youths whom Haines had never seen before. But what a Clarence! Haines scarcely recognized him. Gone was the derby hat. In its stead, the previously immaculate Clarence wore a cap. Gone were the spats; and gone, too, was the little moustache.

"H'ya, coach!" said Clarence breezily. "I hear you need a few extra hands. Well, here we are. Boys, meet Coach Joe Haines. Coach, meet Buzz McPherson, Dunc Malone, and Slippy Wetherby. You've got to make room for us, coach, because we're down here to knock off the Nighthawks tonight, and the whole village of Maple Crossing is along to see us do it. OK by you?"

Haines was a little dazed. After he got his breath back, he said: "But these aren't Riverglen boys, Clarence. If they were the best amateurs on earth, I couldn't get cards for them now."

"They've got cards," chirped Clarence. "They come from Maple Crossing, twenty miles from here, practically in the suburbs. League constitution says bona fide amateurs can play for the team nearest their place of residence. Maple Crossing is thirty miles from Newcastle, forty miles from Lawrence and forty-one miles from Carfax, so they belong to us."

Then Clarence nodded toward his three companions. "Come on, boys; get your skates on and show the boss you know one end of a stick from another."

Haines was pop-eyed with astonishment. This couldn't be Clarence! This breezy, confident fellow couldn't be the elegant nephew of Mrs. Dudley!

"Where the dickens have you been all winter?" blurted the coach.

"Up on my uncle's farm at Maple Crossing," said Clarence, beginning to unlace his shoes. "We heard about the jam you're in, so I got the boys together and we thought we'd come down and give you a hand."

"Can they play hockey?" asked Haines, with a dubious glance at Clarence's three pals.

"They're not bad. They don't get much practice up at

Maple Crossing, of course, for the only other outfit there is the team from Slocum Centre. But we've had a lot of fun this winter. Give us a chance, coach. The folks from the Crossing will be mighty sorry if we don't play. About ten sleigh loads of 'em are coming to town for the game."

"Well," said Haines heavily, thinking of the terrible performances of the recruits he had dug up in Riverglen, "I can't lose."

• • •

IT WAS A weird-looking outfit that Haines iced against the smart Nighthawk squad that night; but, oddly enough, the rink was jammed to the roof, and the crowd let loose an incredible roar of encouragement when the Lions skated out.

Haines hadn't expected a big crowd for that game. Out of common decency, he felt, Riverglen fans would stay at home rather than turn out to watch the massacre.

But they came in droves. Not only that, but the surrounding countryside sent rooters by the sleigh load. Noisiest of them all were the rustic fans from Maple Crossing.

There was a different spirit about that crowd, too. Everyone expected that the Lions would take a licking, but no one seemed downhearted at the prospect. This wasn't any team of imported strangers. These were Riverglen boys and Maple Crossing lads, amateurs every one of 'em, united in common cause. And, by hickory, Riverglen and Maple Crossing meant to root for them—win or lose.

They jeered vociferously when the lordly Nighthawks skated out to limber up; they yelled their heads off when the revamped Lions came out to bat the puck around.

"They might as well holler now," grunted Haines morosely. "They won't have so much to cheer about when this game gets under way."

He was using Clarence at centre on his starting line, flanked by Clark and Pelletier, but he had no confidence in Clarence. Gilroy, tough centre of the Nighthawks, would attend to Clarence. One of Gilroy's famous bodychecks would fix him in short order.

The game got under way. The Nighthawks, jubilant over the unexpected breaks that had put them back in the running and had left the Lions at their mercy, had grinned broadly when they watched the boys from Maple Crossing limbering up. McPherson, Malone, and Wetherby were big fellows, and they looked strong but they were far from fast—downright clumsy, in fact. And Gilroy had laughed outright when he learned who was to face him at centre.

They all remembered Clarence's exhibition in the season's opener.

• • •

AS THE PUCK FELL, Gilroy snapped it up and wheeled away with it. But Clarence pounced on him and batted the puck into the clear, hurdled Gilroy's stick, and broke for the blue line. His pass to Pelletier was intercepted, however, and Wilcox, the Nighthawk right-winger, streaked away on a rush that was stopped at the defence. Clarence picked up the pass-out and headed down mid-ice.

Gilroy was waiting for him. Gilroy never wasted any time in softening up his opponents. He stepped into Clarence heartily and bounced the Lion centre to the ice, rushed, beat the defence, and drilled a hot shot that Henderson stopped.

The Nighthawks were swooping around the Riverglen goal. They had three shots on Henderson in the next few seconds, but Pelletier and Clark were pestering their checks nobly, and all the drives were of the snapshot variety. Then Gilroy, loafing just inside the blue line and waiting for a loose puck, nailed a pass-out from the corner. Just as the puck hit his stick, Gilroy took a forward stride with it, but

Clarence surged out from nowhere and smacked him.

It was a bodycheck that was a bodycheck! Haines could hardly believe his eyes. Clarence hitting back! It was hard to believe, but there was Gilroy sprawled on the ice, and there was Clarence scooting down the ice with the puck while the crowd howled like mad.

Pelletier and Clark pulled up abreast of Clarence as he hit the Nighthawk blue line. A criss-cross play brought Clarence swinging over to right while Clark broke in toward the middle lane and picked up the puck Clarence dropped. The move split the defence, causing the left defence man to involuntarily move out of position to cover Clarence.

Clark swooped in fast and rifled a hard drive at the cage. The goalie sprawled in the net, and his gloved hand lunged desperately at the puck as it spun toward the line. He swept the puck into the clear.

A Nighthawk defence player grabbed it, but Clarence piled into the puck carrier, checked him savagely, and knocked him off balance. Clarence pounced on the rolling disk and let fly. The goalie reached out with his stick in the nick of time and batted the puck out into a milling swarm of players.

Pelletier struggled clear of his check for a fraction of a second. It was all he needed, just long enough to get his stick on the rubber. A quick flip, and it shot over the goalie's head into the net. The crowd went wild. First score to the wrecked, despised Lions! A goal in the first three minutes of play! The din was terrific.

As for Haines, he was too stunned to cheer. The Lions had scored, checked in a neat goal before the Nighthawks had time to get under way. And Clarence, of all people, had paved the way for that tally with two jolting bodychecks.

"Well, I'll be smacked for a row!" muttered Haines solemnly.

• • •

THE LIONS had astonished and delighted their supporters by getting off on the right foot with a quick goal, but it did not take long for the Nighthawks to strike back.

The Nighthawk squad, after all, was a finished hockey machine, and when they got down to serious business, they could make the fur fly. They ripped into the Lions berserk, and launched a series of swift attacks. But what with Clarence hanging onto Gilroy like a limpet, Cassidy and his mate dishing it out on the defence, and Henderson doing flip-flops and handstands in the cage, the visitors couldn't seem to rattle the puck into the twine.

Finally, the Nighthawk coach called in his forwards and sent out the second-line.

"Here's where we get taken," muttered Haines, as he motioned the three rustics from Maple Crossing to the ice.

Now, the Maple Crossing boys were clumsy and lacked polish; but each one of them was as strong as a steer. Years of pitching hay and guiding plows had developed their muscles so that each possessed a shot that could put a dent in a brick wall. And not one of 'em would back down from a fight.

The fast Nighthawk line ran into a barrage of body-checks that sent them back on their heels. McPherson, Malone, and Wetherby weren't so hot when it came to carrying the puck down the ice, but when it came to stopping a puck carrier—well, that was their dish. And every time a Nighthawk was sent on his ear, the delegation from Maple Crossing let out an ear-splitting howl from the gallery.

It had to end some time, however. The Nighthawk right-winger managed to step around Wetherby, race down the boards, and whip a high shot that caromed off the crossbar of the cage. He swooped in between the defence in time to snap up the rebound and then, when Henderson lunged out to smother the return drive, flicked the puck past the sprawling goalie into the cage.

That tied it up, but Haines felt that matters could have been a lot worse. And when the Clarence line came out again and held the Nighthawks in spite of their most determined efforts to score, the coach began to feel actually contented. To be sure, his team wasn't making much of a showing on the attack, but at least they were checking the enemy to a fare-thee-well.

Next time the Maple Crossing trio came out again, the Nighthawks were ready for them, however. They began breaking through, and the Maple Crossing youngsters began swinging at the empty air. Pucks rained on Henderson. He booted them out, batted them out, took them on his pads; but he couldn't stop 'em all. The red light blinked twice before Haines yanked his forwards and sent the Clarence line in again.

Nighthawks 3; Lions 1.

And that was how the scoreboard stood at the end of the period. Haines was quite resigned to defeat, but it was something to know that he had a fighting team out there, anyhow, and he told them so in the dressing room.

"Shucks, we haven't started yet," said Clarence. "Keep on sockin' 'em, fellows, and we'll be ready to take them for a buggy ride in the last period."

"What's come over you all of a sudden?" asked Haines.

"When you were with us at the start of the season I didn't notice you handing out any bodychecks like you gave Gilroy tonight."

"We toughened him up," explained Slippy Wetherby. "When he come up to Maple Crossing, he was too all-fired much of a gentleman to play hockey our style, so I guess we kicked him around a little."

• • •

IN THE SECOND PERIOD, Haines was to learn just how the toughening-up process had taken with Clarence. The Nighthawks had evidently been sent out with instructions to stop fooling and run up a score. Gilroy took a pass from one of his wings, went back around his own net, and came down, picking up speed.

Clarence stepped into him, fair and square. It was a bodycheck that nearly lifted Gilroy out of his pants. He turned a somersault, and then came up, wild-eyed, ready for vengeance.

The puck had gone skittering across to Clark, but before Clarence could get into the play, Gilroy ploughed into him, dumped him flat, giving him a taste of hickory and a knee in the stomach as he did so.

Clarence hopped up, with the crowd yelling murder and the referee blowing his whistle. Off went Clarence's gloves, and he socked Gilroy on the nose. Gilroy replied with a swing that caught Clarence on the ear, but Clarence managed to land another hefty wallop to Gilroy's pan before the players leaped into the battle and dragged them apart.

They both got a stretch in the penalty box, but the crowd was howling its delight. Haines, dazed, scratched his head.

"And that's the little gentleman who let everybody walk all over him a few months ago!" he said.

The Nighthawks, who had come to Riverglen expecting a pushover, found themselves up against a clawing, mauling pack of Lions that wouldn't let up for a moment. These Lions didn't launch many attacks on the enemy goal, but they guarded their own cage as if their lives depended on it.

Gilroy and his wings crashed through for one goal, but they had to earn it. Toward the end of the period, after the Maple Crossing trio had decided that the only way to stop the Nighthawk second line was to check them closer than ever, the Nighthawk manager sent out his first-stringers. They cut loose with a blistering attack.

Henderson was called on to make three hard saves in a row, and then Gilroy broke loose from Clarence, who had been covering him like a blanket. He snared a pass-out from behind the net, and rifled a shot that bounced off Henderson's skate.

No one, least of all the Nighthawks, was prepared for what followed when McPherson, Malone, and Wetherby came out to finish the period. Malone had dumped the Nighthawk centre with a fair-and-square check and went lumbering down the ice. His stickhandling was pathetic, but he managed to get as far as the blue line, with the rival centre overhauling him fast.

Malone didn't even try to reach the defence. He simply lifted that puck in the general direction of the net.

The goalie reached out to catch it in his glove, for it was one of those long shots that are pie for the average net guardian. He caught it, too; but Malone's shot had dynamite in it. The puck seemed to burn right through the goalie's glove. It knocked his arm back, spun out of his grasp; he lunged at it wildly, and then it spun to the ice.

A moment of stunned silence. Then a roar that shook the rink!

"By gosh, I ain't been pitchin' hay all my life for nothin'," said Malone as he skated back.

The score was 4–2 when the teams faced off for the third period.

• • •

HAINES, crouched in the players' box, was tense. Perhaps there was a chance, after all. He thought the Nighthawks looked a little leg-weary. They had been carrying the fight into the enemy's camp all evening and had skated miles for those four goals, taking a terrific thumping and bumping while they were about it.

The thumping and bumping started all over again. The Nighthawks cut loose with two attacks, and every man was ridden hard by his check all the way. They couldn't get a clear shot on Henderson at all. Then they fell back. Their attitude, plainly enough, was: "All right; we've got a two-goal lead, and now we'll protect it."

Clarence had been waiting for that. He wound up around his own net, hit down the middle lane, skates flying. Gilroy made an ineffective lunge at him when he reached centre ice, but Gilroy was all in, and he missed. Clarence streaked down on the defence, faked a pass to Pelletier, slipped the puck across to Clark, dived through the hole in the defence, snagged the return pass ten feet out, and backhanded the disk into the upper left-hand corner for a clean-cut goal.

Riverglen and Maple Crossing went wild: 4–3!

Then the Lions began hitting back. But, after that goal, the Nighthawks tightened up, laid down a barrage of sticks, checked stubbornly.

Then, with the Clarence line on the ice again, and with the clock showing half the period over, came a break; a break for the Nighthawks. It came in a wild scrimmage around the Nighthawk net, when Clarence had brought the puck in for a shot on goal and his wings had stormed in, hoping to grab a rebound, a loose puck, a pass, anything that might give them a chance to tie it up. Haines saw Gilroy come tumbling out of the fracas and go sprawling on the ice.

The whistle blew. The referee was thumbing someone to the bench.

It was Clarence. He looked particularly glum as he skated over toward the penalty box.

"Sorry, coach," he said. "Accidental trip."

"That's torn it," muttered Haines.

With the one-man advantage, the Nighthawks tore into the Lions with a rush that saw half a dozen players sprawled on the ice in front of Henderson's cage, but with Henderson lying beside the net with the puck buried beneath his sweater.

Cassidy batted the puck down the ice after the faceoff, but Gilroy and his wings got organized and came down again, reinforced by an extra forward, leaving a lone defenceman back of their blue line.

In they came, swift as swallows. Gilroy faked a shot, then drifted a pass to his right wing.

Pelletier's long stick came out, deflected the puck just in time, and then the wingman was in full stride, scooping it up and on his way. The Nighthawks went streaming in pursuit, but they would have needed wings to catch Pelletier, the fastest skater in the league. He went storming in on the luckless defenceman, sifted around him, streaked in on the cage.

The goalie came out to meet him. Pelletier held his shot, made his move. The goalie lunged forward in an effort to smother the shot. Pelletier zipped the rubber into the empty net.

"Tied, by golly!" howled Haines, now as wild-eyed with excitement as any fan in the rink. "Let's go!"

The Nighthawks couldn't play a defensive game now. To tie up the series, they had to win. They had gambled with that odd goal, and they had lost it. Down they came, desperate.

Haines sent out his relief forwards. The hands of the

clock were creeping around. Five minutes to go. Clarence, long since out of the penalty box, nudged Haines.

"Here's where we take them, coach," observed Clarence. "Lemme at 'em!"

Haines sent out his first-string forwards when there was an offside faceoff at the Lions' blue line. Clarence won the draw, snapped up the puck, and went back behind his own net. He came swinging around the corner.

Clark had been covering Gilroy, but suddenly the rival centre broke away and lunged in. His stick flashed out as Clarence came beyond the net. It all happened so quickly that Clarence was caught flat-footed. The puck was knocked away, went spinning through the air toward the cage.

How Henderson covered up in time to trap the puck between the upright and his pads always remained a mystery to Haines. The goalie did it, and then fell on it.

That meant a faceoff right beside the Riverglen goal. Haines scarcely dared look.

The puck fell. Sticks clashed. And then the puck went skimming away off down the ice with half a dozen forwards wheeling away in wild pursuit.

Gilroy reached it first, but his stick was hardly on the rubber when Clarence came racing up behind him, hooked the puck away, and passed over to Clark almost in the same motion. Clark let drive for the backboards.

The puck came bounding out at an angle. Clarence wiggled through to scoop up the puck, saw the goalie hugging the side of the cage, snapped up the disk, and went around the net. The goalie plunged back, sprawled on the ice to guard the other side. Clarence saw Clark break clear from Gilroy. He drilled the puck across. Clark made no mistake. He slammed the rubber high into the twine for the deciding goal.

That was the end. The leg-weary and discouraged Nighthawks went to pieces in the remaining minutes of the game. The gong rang to proclaim the Lions champions of the league. The crowd swarmed onto the ice and carried them to the dressing room.

Haines had a hard time rescuing Clarence. The crowd seemed bent on tearing his sweater to pieces for souvenirs. But in the safety of the dressing room he extended his hand.

"Thanks, son," said the coach. "I reckon I misjudged you a little. Winnin' that title means a lot to Riverglen, I guess, but it meant a lot to me, too."

Clarence grinned. "Listen, coach," he said. "I want you to do something for me. If you ever catch me taking a bumping without trying to hand out a receipt for it—"

"I'll send you back to Maple Crossing," interrupted Haines solemnly. "By the way, Clarence, what did they do to you up there?"

Clarence was thoughtful for a moment. Then he winked at Haines.

"I'd hate to tell you, coach!" he said, wagging his head. "But if you want to play hockey with those birds, you've got to go through the mill. But once you learn to hit back— why, they're a fine crowd. Boy—they can sure knock a lot of the gloss off a gentleman up in that man's burg!"

PEPPER POT

T HE WILD WAR WHOOP of young Steve Regan cut through the yammering roar of the crowd. Every fan and player in the H&F League knew that yell. You heard it whenever the Farmstead Bobcats were in a tough spot and needed rallying—which meant that you heard it often enough if you followed the Bobcats!

Whenever Regan cut loose with that yell he fairly danced on his skates; he brandished his stick, flung back his head and let go from both lungs:

"Eeeeeee-yaow!"

It was supposed to be an imitation of a bobcat's scream, and that ear-splitting squawk served notice to the Bobcat forwards that Regan was back on defence again and spoiling for battle. It served notice to the fans that the Bobcats weren't licked yet, even if it was the third period and their old enemies, the Hanfield Rovers, were leading by a couple of goals. Not so far as Regan was concerned anyhow.

"Shake it up! Shake it up! Come on now—step into 'em!"

Regan's urgent chatter didn't let up for a second. The forward line stiffened as the Rovers came down, but a Rover wing slipped through on the left boards and beat his check to a forward pass.

"Nail him, Johnny!" bawled Regan, as the puck carrier raced across the blue line.

Johnny Hooper, his defencemate, aimed a lusty body-check at the Rover player, who sidestepped and went around. Johnny went into a tailspin and sprawled ingloriously on the ice.

But Regan was backing up the play. He cut loose with another nerve-shattering yell as he caught the Rover off stride, nailed him amidships and smeared him over three square yards of ice.

"Gangway!" he yowled and snapped up the puck, high-tailed it up over the blue line.

Clyde Harper, the Bobcat centre, swung around smoothly and struck out for the Rover blue line. A slick, streamlined skater, every movement seemed effortless. As for Regan, pushing the puck ahead of him, skating in a crouch with awkward, choppy strokes, he was about as graceful as a calf moose in a bog. A rover swooped alongside to check him and Regan fired the puck ahead.

Harper had to reach for it. But he trapped the puck

casually just before it went over the line, just as if Regan had placed it right on his stick blade instead of five feet off the mark. Then he tricked his way inside, squirmed around a defenceman, worked his way in close, and flipped the puck at the net.

An innocent, easy shot, but it came so close it made the crowd gasp. It ticked off the post into the back screen. And by that time young Steve Regan was barging in after it.

Regan and a big defenceman slammed into each other and up against the board with a smash. The puck came skimming out as Regan sprawled on the ice, slashing it across with his stick. Harper, right on the crease, flipped it disdainfully into the cage.

But the referee paid no attention to the blinking goal light. He swooped in, picked up the puck and skated over beside the net.

"You were in the crease," he told Harper, shaking his head.

Harper shrugged. But Steve Regan cut loose with a bellow of fury. He streaked across to the official, sizzling mad.

"What's that? He wasn't in the crease! A fair pass—right on the line!"

Regan waved his arms. He yelled. He argued. He danced with wrath. The referee just grinned and shook his head. As for Clyde Harper, he stood by, smiling thinly, as if it didn't matter one way or the other. Tall, fair-haired and handsome, smoothest skater and trickiest stick handler the Bobcats ever had, star of the team, Harper didn't argue with referees.

"What does it get you?" he often said. "Ever hear of a referee reversing himself? I save my breath."

Some of the Bobcats gathered around Regan and pushed him away when the referee began making threatening motions toward the penalty box. Regan went back to his position, reluctantly. The crowd jeered. He glared up at them and the raspberry thundered down like an avalanche.

• • •

UP IN THE FIFTH ROW, just above the penalty box, Mr. Skates Kelsey watched all this with profound interest.

He was a paunchy man with a florid, rubbery face, a bulbous nose and shrewd blue eyes. His felt hat, perched on the extreme back of his head, looked as if it had been sat on, which was the case. His collar was rumpled and he was chewing a dead cigar. Mr. Kelsey did not look famous, nor did he look important. In the hockey world, however, he was both.

"Whaddaya think of him, Skates? Whaddaya think?" begged the man beside him.

Kelsey shifted the cigar and glanced at his companion, a thin-faced, well-groomed individual in a derby hat.

"Which one?" he grunted in a husky bass.

"Why, Spike Randall, of course. Who do you think? Haven't I been pointing him out to you all night?"

"Yeah." Kelsey nodded wearily. The man in the derby hat was Lattimer, secretary of the Hanfield team and he had coaxed Kelsey all the way up here to the sticks for a peek at a centre he had touted as being the hottest prospect since Apps. "Yeah, he looks all right," Kelsey repeated.

Play was on again. He watched Randall, the Rover centre, work down the middle lane. He saw the pint-sized Regan try to step into Randall. He saw Regan miss and go headlong. But he saw Clyde Harper slip smoothly in and pick the puck off Randall's stick, saw Harper sift back down toward the Rover goal.

"See how he sidestepped that bodycheck. See how—"

Kelsey grunted. "Randall is all right," he said. "He's big and he can skate and he can carry the puck without falling on his face. But for big-time hockey—"

Kelsey's silence said plenty.

"No?" Lattimer questioned painfully.

"No."

The Rover secretary looked disappointed. "That's too bad. I was sure you'd like Randall. We think a lot of him up here. I thought you'd want to grab him for the Chiefs right away."

"We've got fifty prospects just as good as Randall. Some of 'em better. Prospects we tabbed two, three and four years back when they were only junior age."

"Then why do the Chiefs need a scout at all?"

"My boss," said Kelsey heavily, "has made that selfsame remark. More than once!"

He watched the game again. Randall had the puck behind the Rover goal and was coming out with it. He crossed the blue line. Clyde Harper took a casual lunge at him but Randall slipped past. Harper didn't chase him but ambled up to the blue line instead.

It was young Steve Regan who stopped Randall. Dumped him hard and solid, grabbed the puck, hopped up the ice half a dozen paces and drilled the puck all the way over to Harper at the far blue line.

Harper picked his way inside and flipped the puck, turning away. He didn't even look back as the light flashed.

"One thing about that Harper," muttered the Rover secretary grudgingly, "he sure makes it look easy. He's smooth."

"Tell you another guy who makes it look easy; Nels Stewart, 'Ole Poison.' There's a guy who lasted years in the big time and got himself a hatful of goals."

Lattimer was thoughtful. He sensed that Kelsey was interested in what was going on down there. And classing Harper with Nels Stewart! Wow!

"If the Bobcats win this game tonight does it tie up the league?" asked Kelsey.

"Yep. With the deciding game back in Farmstead. Don't worry," grinned Lattimer. "They won't tie it. Why it must be fifteen years since Farmstead took a league title from us—"

The smile left his face. A Bobcat forward broke through to the corner and fired a pass that slid right across the goal mouth. The Rover goalie fell all over himself trying to clear it, got tangled up, and went down. Clyde Harper took one lazy stride and slapped at the puck. It bounced into the cage.

"Eeeeeee-yaow!" squalled Steve Regan, the squat, cocky, red-headed bantam back on defence. The score was tied. And when the Rovers hustled to try to snare the winning goal in the remaining few minutes of time, Regan yelled his head off.

He was all over the defence area. Bodychecking opponents twice as big as himself. Piling into the corners. Hoofing the puck out to the blue line.

The Bobcats were beginning to weaken under the pressure. But not Regan.

"Lay into 'em, gang!" he howled. He was the scrappiest man on the ice. During a faceoff the Bobcat coach beckoned Regan in. The carrot-thatched defenceman scrambled over to the fence bellowing with indignation. The argument with the coach was brief and bitter. Regan stayed on.

The going got rough. The referee was letting a lot get by; the sly butt-end to the ribs, the knee, the elbow. Hardboiled hockey! Randall sifted down on a three-man attack and went into the corner after a loose puck. Regan dove after him like a terrier, fought for the puck. Randall pivoted sharply and drove the kid smash into the boards.

It was rough stuff. But the whistle didn't blow. And Regan didn't stay down either. He fairly bounced out of the corner. And he bounced swinging. Randall towered over him but Regan was bursting with fight. He missed Randall's jaw with a haymaker—and the big centre grabbed him. They went down battling.

"Tough little rooster, huh?" said Lattimer.

"Nice time to get a penalty," grunted Kelsey sourly. "Quarrelsome brat! Argues with referees. Gets penalties with the score tied."

"He makes a lot of noise for the size of him."

"Noise don't get goals. You see him get any goals tonight?"

Regan went to the penalty box, still spluttering wrathfully. But Randall went with him.

And with Randall went the Rovers punch. They sagged.

"Come on, gang! Step into 'em. You there, Johnny—get going!" shrieked the fiery-headed Regan. Even in the penalty box he could still holler.

The Bobcats ganged. They stormed in. It was Johnny Hooper who paved the way for the winning goal after a wild melee in front of the cage. It was Johnny's shot that bounced in front of the crease with Johnny and two other players sprawled on the ice, the goalie floundering after the stop. Clyde Harper picked it up and scooped it in, as disdainfully as if he were at practice.

The Bobcats hugged each other. Young Steve Regan fell out of the penalty box in his glee, whooping hoarsely. But Harper skated off the ice looking bored.

"Cool as a cucumber, by gosh!" said Lattimer in grudging admiration.

"Yeah. Nice player," mumbled Kelsey. Then he added with an air of indifference, "They play back in Farmstead on Thursday, huh?"

"Thursday night. But we'll take 'em. They've never snaffled the title yet. We'll take 'em," predicted Lattimer.

"Ought to be a good game. Too bad you have to go back to the city."

"Yeah. Too bad." Kelsey yawned.

Lattimer was very thoughtful as he pushed his way toward the dressing room after the game was over.

"Pretty cagy! A mighty cagy customer!" mused Lattimer. "But he didn't fool me. No, sir! Not a bit."

• • •

THE HANFIELD & Farmstead League—otherwise known as the H&F or Hay-and-Feed Circuit—was strictly amateur and strictly bush league. A five-team set-up in the barnyard loop, its teams had no higher aspiration than the Joshua P. Wiggins Trophy, a small and far from costly mug, emblematic of the league title. When the Wiggins Trophy was duly won, hockey in the H&F League was finished for the year. The boys could spend the rest of the season listening to big-time games on the radio.

Farmstead had three thousand people and at least twenty-nine hundred of them talked hockey all day Thursday. The remaining hundred, being infants in arms, took little interest. By beating Hanfield on Hanfield's own ice the Bobcats had a chance to collar the Wiggins Trophy for the first time in the history of the league.

Steve Regan checked out of the Harper hardware store at six o'clock and hustled home to supper. Young Dan, his brother, was busy stowing away a large helping of stew and talking to his mother when Steve came in.

"Sure, it's a mean trick, but what do you expect, Ma?" Dan was saying. "It ain't fair, but old John Harper is like that."

"Like what? And what's a mean trick?" demanded Steve.

Dan looked guilty. He was fourteen, cocky and aggressive, a fiery-thatched second edition of his brother. "Nothing," he mumbled.

Steve noticed that his mother looked disturbed. "Sorry, Ma," he grinned, taking his plate from her before she could heap it too high. "I've got to get up from the table hungry if we're going to win a hockey game tonight. Boy!" He sat down, sniffing appreciatively. "Smells good. Now what's all this about somebody playing a mean trick on someone?"

Dan wriggled. "I'll tell you tomorrow."

"You'll tell me now. Out with it."

"I was talking to Harper's bookkeeper on the way home tonight. He says you're going to be let out at the end of next week."

There was a dead silence. Soberly, Steve munched beef and potatoes. Mrs. Regan said, "Maybe it's just talk. Don't worry about it, Steve."

"I'm offered a job in Hanfield last fall," mused Steve, "so John Harper says he needs a bright young man to learn the hardware business. Permanent job. Big opportunity. And the hockey crowd says it's mighty swell of him because it keeps me in town so I can play for the team."

"And the minute the hockey season is over, out you go on your ear," exploded Dan. "The Hanfield job would have been good for all the year round. Now that the hockey season is over old man Harper doesn't care if you starve all summer."

Steve shrugged. "Nice way to do business. So he's going to break the news next week. I'm not supposed to know about it just now."

"Holy cats, no. He'd be afraid you'd walk out on the team." Dan was alarmed. "You won't let it make any difference will you, Steve? I know I shouldn't have told you."

"How do you mean, difference?"

"I mean—well, gosh hang it—we've just *got* to beat the Rovers tonight. If you get mad—and I wouldn't blame you, mind—if you get mad and just say to hang with the Bobcats—"

Steve gave him a look. "I'm not that kind of hockey player," he grunted.

His brother sighed with relief. "I know darn well you're not. But just the same, you're kinda hot-tempered like me and I was scared you'd maybe walk out on 'em."

"Don't worry. I've been dreaming about helping bring that Wiggins Trophy to town ever since I could wear skates."

"And I suppose if the Bobcats do win it," ventured his mother, "Mr. Harper will take all the credit. To hear him talk, Clyde is the only player on the team who knows one end of a stick from the other."

"That's not bothering me either," said Steve. "There are only two things I've ever wanted in hockey and one is to see the Bobcats win this league."

"What's the other?" Dan asked.

"Well, I've always kind of hankered to make the grade with a pro team. I guess every hockey player has that notion. But how are you going to do it, buried up here in the sticks where the big fellows never hear of you and never get a look at you? So that's out. But we're gonna win that cup tonight, no foolin', job or no job."

"That's talking!" applauded Dan. He gulped down a cup of coffee and snatched up his coat. "I'm on my way. That rink will be packed to the rafters tonight and I'll have to get in line early if I want a front seat."

He scrambled out. The door slammed. Mrs. Regan put a hand on Steve's shoulder.

"Don't worry about the job, son. Something will turn up."

"Sure. It always does. I pried a reserved seat ticket out of 'em for you, Ma. It's on the sideboard."

"You just play the best you can. I think you're a better player than Clyde Harper anyhow. I don't care what anyone says."

"Whoa, now! Whoa! He's a swell player. Best man on the team, I'd say, even if I don't like him much. Look at the goals he gets. He's as near a big-time player as we've ever had in this burg, and it's a funny thing to me that some of the pro teams haven't grabbed him long ago."

"Well, I don't like him," said Mrs. Regan decidedly. "He's too conceited. The only reason Mr. Harper supported the team this winter was to give Clyde a chance to show off."

• • •

WHEN STEVE CAME into the Bobcat dressing room that night he knew something had happened. The atmosphere was tense, of course, but that was to be expected. Farmstead didn't come within inches of the league title every year. Yet there was something else. Clyde Harper, for instance, didn't look as bored and indifferent as usual. He seemed actually excited. And the other lads, getting into their gear, were gaping at him as enviously as if he had just won a sweepstake.

". . . all I know is that he's supposed to be here tonight to look me over again," Harper was saying. "It was Lattimer himself who tipped me off. Mighty thoughtful of him, I'd say."

"You be careful of what that guy Lattimer tells you," growled Jim Bell, manager of the Bobcats. "He isn't trying to do this team any favours."

"Think he was just stringing me?" retorted Harper. "What good would that do him. He said Kelsey originally came up to have a look at Randall. He couldn't see Randall as a prospect but when he saw me play he got interested."

"Skates Kelsey? Scout for the Chiefs?" spoke up Steve Regan. "What's this about?"

"Kelsey saw the game the other night. Just because I was lucky enough to get a few goals he seemed to think maybe I had something," said Harper smugly. "Of course, I won't be disappointed if nothing comes of it, but still—I'll sure be out there doing my stuff tonight."

Steve began taking off his shoes. He was thoughtful. After Harper clumped out of the room in full gear, he edged over to Jim Bell.

"That right about Skates Kelsey being here tonight?"

"I think it's a gag myself," grunted the manager. "But I was talking to Lattimer a few minutes ago and he swore it was true."

"Why should Lattimer go out of his way to tell us a big-time scout is going to watch us? Isn't he afraid it'll make us so hot we'll climb all over his Rovers?"

"I thought of that," Bell admitted. "But Lattimer is smart. He may figure we don't need a big-time scout or anything else to make us as hot as we'll ever be for this game. On the other hand, telling Clyde Harper that the scout will be watching *him*—I don't like it."

Steve nodded. "Maybe you're right."

"Harper thinks pretty well of himself at any time. This'll make his head swell up like a balloon, or I don't know the signs. And maybe it'll give the other fellows notions too." Bell turned a sour look on Steve. "Don't you go gettin' ideas. Kelsey ain't interested in you."

"Did he say so?"

Bell nodded.

"Thought you made too much noise and got too few goals. 'Noise don't get goals,' he told Lattimer. And that penalty you got in the last few minutes of play didn't go down with him."

"I'm supposed to let Randall mow me down and let him get away with it!" yelped Steve hotly. "The referee was letting them get away with murder. Besides, it took Randall out of the game, didn't it?"

"Well, he didn't like it. Far as I'm concerned I thought you played a good, hard game. You hold this whole team together by my way of figuring. But maybe these big-timers look at things different."

Steve got into skates and uniform. Bell glanced at him sharply as he was going out, then followed him into the corridor. He slapped a friendly hand on Steve's shoulder.

"Don't look so blue, kid. You gotta admit Harper has plenty on the ball. He makes it look so blamed easy. Lattimer said that's what caught Kelsey's eye. Harper seems to be playin' under wraps all the time. Kelsey said he reminded him of Nels Stewart."

"Best player we've ever had around these parts," Steve said gruffly "I'm not blue, Jim. A little disappointed, I guess. That crack about me being too noisy—"

"Forget it. Yell all you like. We can't all make the big time, Steve. I had ideas that way myself once. Main thing is to do as good as you can in the league you're in."

Steve clumped down the ramp and through the gate. Usually he announced his presence with a yip and a yell. It wasn't show-off stuff; when he felt ice under his skates, heard the buzz of a gathering crowd, and smelled the atmosphere of an impending game, he felt so full of pep he simply had to let off steam. But tonight he slipped out silently, unsmiling.

He batted the puck around, tossed potshots at the goalie, got limbered up. He watched Harper pick up the puck and go in. Easy and effortless; Harper scarcely seemed to be trying. *Flick!* A loose, careless motion and the puck was in the net.

Harper wheeled away, but he had one eye on the crowd. The story about Harper's big league prospects would be getting around by now.

"What's the matter?" Johnny Hooper nudged Steve's ribs. "You're quiet as a clam."

"Nothing to holler about—yet."

"Don't let it get you nervous. This is our big night," grinned Johnny.

That was the way the crowd felt about it too. They had

come all set to celebrate a Bobcat victory. They had come with cowbells and horns. A Bobcat win would set loose the biggest uproar in Farmstead since 1918. But, right now, as the fans clattered to their seats, there was tension. It hung over the rink. Farmstead had come close to that title so often and had been so often denied. It would be a killer if they missed this time.

The Bobcats went back to the dressing room to await the whistle.

At the gate Jim Bell said to Steve, "Lattimer wasn't kidding. He's here all right."

The manager indicated a middle-aged, sloppily dressed man with a ruddy face and a bulbous nose, sitting a few rows back of the penalty box. "Steve, that's the famous Skates Kelsey."

Steve looked, with considerable awe. Famous folk were not often seen in Farmstead. It was hard to believe that the untidy man in the battered felt hat was the great Kelsey, the scout who had opened the gates to a big-time career for players whose names were now known to hockey fans all over the country.

"Registered at the hotel under the name of Johnson," grunted Bell. "But it's Kelsey all right. Saw him once about ten years ago. I'd know his hide in a tannery."

The teams got rolling. Tense, tight hockey. Attack and counter attack, with the crowd alternately holding its breath and screaming.

Randall, of the Rovers, broke through and bore down on the defence. There was a time when Steve Regan would have come out with a whoop and a roar to smack Randall with everything but the water bucket. This time was different. He blocked Randall out of the play and steered him off to the corner. Efficiently. Unhurriedly. And when he got hold of the puck he flipped it carelessly up to Clyde Harper at the blue line without so much as a yell.

Harper went through alone, ignoring his wings. A smooth, brilliant rush that split the defence and brought the Rover goalie out. The Bobcats might have scored if Harper had made a play to one of his wings instead of trying it solo. As it was, the goalie barely blocked the shot and Harper got a big hand. He shrugged and skated backward to await the counterattack.

Back came the Rovers. And this time it was Tim Reddick, Bobcat left-winger, who broke up the rush. Tim's specialty was stick handling. He could kill off penalties with the best of them. Now he proceeded to stage an exhibition of his art. Weaving trickily in the mid-ice area he circled back and forth, evading every Rover who came in to check him.

Fancy stuff. But it wasn't getting the Bobcats anywhere. And when Tim finally lost the puck to Randall he glanced over toward the back area of the penalty box proudly. With a big-league scout in the stands, Tim was putting his best foot foremost.

In the second period the Rovers struck hard. They lashed out with an attack that brought them swarming inside the Bobcat defence zone. Steve Regan met them grimly. He blocked. He bodied. He cleared rebounds. He attended to business like a veteran. But carefully. None of those riotous, abandoned bodychecks that could earn you a penalty if you connected the wrong way. And when a Rover charged him with a high stick Steve merely side-stepped instead of handing back punishment. Stay on the ice! Stay out of the penalty box! And keep quiet. Noise doesn't get goals.

Keeping his mouth shut didn't get them either, for that matter. Or keep them out. Halfway through the period the Rovers smashed through and tallied from a wild melee of flashing skates, flying sticks, and plunging bodies.

It was when the Bobcats were on the short end of the score that Steve's war whoops usually rang the loudest. But not this night. Grim and tight-lipped, he crouched as the puck was faced at centre.

Over on the Rover bench Mr. Lattimer smiled gleefully.

"We got 'em!" he said to the Rover coach. "They're not clicking. Every man-jack of 'em has one eye on the puck and the other on the crowd."

Up back of the penalty box, Skates Kelsey slouched down a little farther in his seat. Kelsey was frowning. Doubtfully he eyed Steve Regan down there on the Bobcat defence.

"Wrong again," muttered Kelsey.

Tim Reddick had the puck, was working his way down the wing.

"Pass it over!" yapped Clyde Harper. He rapped his stick sharply on the ice. Reddick, stubbornly hanging onto the puck, went on up. He got into trouble at the defence and the puck came flying out. Harper banged at it savagely, wide of the net, and wheeled without trying to bore in.

There were noisy ructions in the Bobcat dressing room when the period was over.

"What are you fellows trying to do to me?" Harper exploded wrathfully. "A big-league scout comes all the way up here to look me over and you all lie down. How can I get goals if you don't work with me on my plays?"

"How about you layin' one down once in a while?" yelled Tim Reddick. "That's what you're there for. You're not the only guy on this team, Mr. Big!"

Harper wanted to fight. Jim Bell, sweating with anxiety, held the pair apart.

"Holy cats, fellows!" he begged. "Get down to business, will you? If you can't pull up your socks in this period, you're sunk. These guys are licking you."

They knew it. Everybody knew it. And the knowledge that the title, so long awaited, so close to their grasp, was slipping away with every passing minute, made them jittery. Sulky and desperate, they trooped out for the last period.

They held the oncoming Rovers out for five minutes. And then Randall pulled one of his solo rushes from back of the Rover goal. He raced down, blades flashing, swept across the blue line.

Steve Regan edged over to meet him. A neat, smartly-timed bodycheck, the way a big-leaguer would do it.

A shift of the hip, however, and Randall brushed past him. Right in on the goal. Floundering, Steve saw Randall swoop right in on the crease and slam the puck high into the rigging.

Rovers 2; Bobcats 0.

The crowd groaned.

Steve set his jaw. The Bobcat forward line was wavering. Harper looked fed up and disgusted. A moment after the faceoff, the puck came skimming back toward the blue line. Steve raced up for it, snagged it, kept right on going. He could rush when he had to. He shifted down the right alley, played the boards, tore past the Rover left-winger, snapped up the puck on the rebound, and cut in sharply at the blue line. A shift carried him through the defence. He was inside.

Regan's shot on goal—when he got one—was usually a blazing, blasting, wild-eyed affair that either knocked the goalie down or hit the back of the rink like a six-inch shell. But not this one. Regan had been studying that casual, effortless shot of Harper's. The stuff that caught the eye of a big-league scout.

He swerved in front of the net and ticked the puck casually. Just a flip. He swung away, his face studiously expressionless, a study in boredom. And then, with the groan of the crowd, he looked back. The puck was skittering over to the corner, where it had bounced off the goalie's stick. Jim Bell called him in at the next change of players. Steve sat on the bench, stony-eyed. Gloom hung over the bench and over the crowd in dark and soggy gobs.

The Rovers smashed in again. The Bobcats had lost their punch. Disorganized, they battled gamely but feebly to keep the puck out of their defence zone. But the Rovers had the whip hand and knew it. The puck whizzed past the goal post, bounded out. Randall swooped in. The puck thudded into the goalie's pads and the goalie sprawled, hanging onto the rubber.

"Let me out there, Jim," muttered Steve Regan as the whistle blew. He heaved himself over the fence without waiting for the word.

"Eeeeeee-yaow!" The good old Regan war whoop, that maniacal screech that had been a Bobcat battle cry all season, echoed to the rafters. And a red-thatched fireball swooped over in front of the net for the faceoff. "Come on, gang!" he bawled. "What are we waitin' for? Let's get going!"

The puck fell. *Bam!* Steve smacked into the nearest Rover, all knees, elbows, and stick, dumped him lustily. He pounced on the puck and banged it over to Clyde Harper. "Take it down! G'wan with it!"

Harper didn't get far. The Rovers surged back. Steve was all over the place, whooping. A Rover who tried to cross-check him got smashed into the boards.

The wilting Bobcats stiffened. Just a little. But they were showing fight. Anybody would fight with that war whoop urging them.

"G'wan up with him, Tim! Give him the old pass. Attaboy!" bawled Regan. And Reddick was off with Clyde Harper, sifting toward the Rover blue line. They didn't make it that time but it was close. And when the Rovers came back Steve didn't wait. He met the puck carrier at the blue line and got the puck somehow, took it down, and drove it hard from outside the defence. A miss, but it shaved the post, sent the Rover goalie ducking frantically, and hit the back boards with a smash like a cannon ball.

The team began to knit. The Bobcats were fighting again. The crowd, with no goals to cheer for, was in an uproar anyhow. Steve was tearing in after that rebound. He smashed into a defenceman at the boards; they went down with a crash. He came out of it with the puck, stickhandled his way past a forward, got into shooting position, and let drive.

No funny little flip shot this time. A blistering, savage shot that almost tore through the back of the net. And when the light blinked, Steve flung his stick in the air and shrieked, "Eeeeeee-yaow!"

Moments later, he tore in after a rebound and a Rover defenceman met him fair and square with an elbow in the teeth. Steve dropped his stick and answered with a smacking left to the jaw. The whistle shrilled. The referee waved them both to the bench. But it meant that the Bobcats were fighting now and Steve Regan didn't give a hoot whether Skates Kelsey saw him get the penalty or not.

"I don't take that from anybody, see. Penalty or no penalty," he growled at the Rover as he skated off.

But it was the Rovers who were thrown right back in on their own doorstep while the teams were battling five men to a side. And two minutes after the penalty was served Clyde Harper picked up Steve's long pass, with its warning roar of "Build it up!" and flashed into Rover territory. A pass to Reddick, a swift shuttling of movement, and then Harper broke through just as the return pass came across.

He flicked it neatly into the net and the score was tied. But even Harper was human. He actually grinned as he skated back. The rink was like a madhouse. Every horn and cowbell in the place was going full blast.

The Bobcats were rolling. It was Reddick who snagged the winning goal three minutes later but everybody had a part in it. Most of all Steve Regan, spark-plugging the whole crew, playing his old clumsy, noisy, two-fisted, fighting game that kept them humping and made them a team. Who cared if it was big-league or not? The Bobcats had won!

They were still celebrating in the dressing room when Skates Kelsey shambled in. Clyde Harper smirked expectantly and cast a proud look upon his teammates. But Kelsey walked over to Steve.

"My name's Kelsey," he grumbled. "I hunt ivory for the Chiefs. We're bringin' up a guy from our farm club. Defenceman. Spark Plug. Pepper Pot. We need a fella to take his place. Like to come down for a tryout?"

Steve's mouth opened. He goggled. He tried to speak. At last he managed it.

"Me?"

"Why not? You got some things to learn. A little crude yet. But you got fight. Hockey heart, see. Watched you spark this team the other night so I come over to look at you again—"

Skates Kelsey frowned. Then he exploded as he continued.

"Listen, kid. What in the hell *was* the matter with you tonight? I thought you'd never get goin'."

Steve gulped.

"Why . . . why nothing much, Mr. Kelsey. I guess I just wasn't myself for a while."

HOMETOWN HERO

E VERY TIME SKATES KELSEY went broke, he made himself a solemn promise to reform. No more betting on the gee-gees. No more sitting up all night with the pretty pasteboards or the galloping dominoes. And no more liquor.

"Never again!" groaned Skates, as he sat dolefully on a sagging bed in a small-town hotel that winter evening.

This time, he meant it. He always did.

But whenever he got himself into one of these jams, there was a way out. He could always send a telegram to the business office of the Chiefs, big-league hockey team, and the long-suffering business manager would wire the erring scout an advance on salary.

But that way out was now closed. He had used it once too often.

Skates glumly surveyed the contents of his pockets, which he had emptied onto the dingy counterpane of the bed: one empty match box, a bunch of keys, a corkscrew, a crumpled ace of clubs, a handkerchief that needed a bath, half a dozen old letters, two lead pencils, and a couple of telegrams. No money—and no railway ticket.

One of the telegrams read:

WE HAVE COVERED YOUR BUM CHECK AS REQUESTED BY YOUR COLLECT WIRE OF TUESDAY AND CREDITED SAME TO COVER ONE MONTH'S SALARY IN LIEU OF NOTICE STOP YOU ARE NOW FIRED STOP HARRON STOP PRESIDENT

To which Skates Kelsey had replied, collect:

YES STOP BUT HOW AM I TO GET HOME STOP

Harron's answer was there on the bed:

YOUR TRANSPORTATION NO LONGER PROBLEM OF THIS CLUB PRAISE BE STOP TRY WALKING YOU NO GOOD LOAFER STOP ANY MORE COLLECT WIRES WILL BOUNCE BACK FASTER THAN ONE OF YOUR OWN CHEQUES STOP HARRON

So that was that! Skates Kelsey shut his eyes and shuddered.

He got up and moved over toward the window. Snowflakes were falling gently and silently beyond the pane.

Mr. Kelsey, in dressing gown and pyjamas, turned away from the window. The room was chilly and he was aware that he was hungry. He ran his fingers through his thinning sandy hair and pondered the problem of what to do when one is stranded without job or money in a one-horse lumber town.

He had arrived in Wheelsburg considerably the worse for wear, and on the principle that one may as well be hanged for a sheep as for a lamb, his first move had been to send his suit out to be cleaned and pressed. He had thrown in his hat, too, for repairs.

It occurred to him now that it might cause talk at the clerk's desk if he failed to tip the boy. So he took a pad of notepaper from his grip, sat down at the unsteady desk, uncapped his fountain pen and wrote the figure 4 at the top of the first blank page.

After a moment, he added: "All the boys on the team send their best wishes. Hope we see you again soon. Your old pal, Charlie Warner."

Mr. Kelsey blotted this carefully, tore out the page, folded it and thrust it into one of the letters on the bed. He was a short, paunchy man with a rubbery, good-humoured face, traced with the purplish veins of high living and illuminated by a bulbous nose. Everyone said that Skates Kelsey was his own worst enemy.

• • •

HE WAS LOOKING out the window again and vainly trying to think of someone to whom he could wire for funds when there was a knock at the door. The hotel's bellhop came in with his suit and hat.

"Here y'are, Mr. Kelsey."

"Thank you, son. Thank you," replied Skates Kelsey benevolently. "Put it on the bill." Then with a grand gesture: "Wait a minute! Wait a minute! A little tip for yourself."

He opened a bureau drawer, as if seeking silver, and then he turned. "Hockey fan?" he inquired, with a twinkle in his eye.

Mr. Kelsey had guessed right. He usually did. The bellhop, with big ears and buckteeth, confessed that hockey fans didn't come any hotter.

"You're the scout for the Chiefs, ain't you, Mr. Kelsey? Minute I saw your name on the register I said to Al—he's the clerk—I said, 'Why, that's Skates Kelsey, the old big-league defence.' I said to him, 'I betcha the Chiefs sent him to look at Tim Cardigan—'"

"You guessed right, my boy," interrupted Skates Kelsey. "And seeing you're a hockey fan, I'll ask you something. Which would you rather have, a small tip for delivering my suit, or an autograph of Charlie Warner?"

The lad's eyes bulged. "Charlie Warner! A real autograph, in his own writin'?"

"His own authentic signature," replied Mr. Kelsey. "I had a letter from good old Charlie just yesterday. Now, let me see—where did I put that letter? Ah, here it is!"

"Gosh!" exclaimed the boy reverently. "I'd give my shirt for Charlie Warner's autograph. Boy! Wait till I tell the fellows I've got that! Centre for the Chiefs, Charlie Warner himself."

Mr. Kelsey handed the lad the page he had written a few minutes previously and the bellhop nearly expired with gratitude.

"You're goin' to the game tonight, ain'tcha, Mr. Kelsey?"

"Game?"

"Sure. Didn't you come up to look at Tim Cardigan?"

• • •

SKATES KELSEY SMILED mysteriously. He had never heard of Tim Cardigan in his life; he didn't even know Wheelsburg had a hockey team. The only reason he was staying in Wheelsburg was because he hadn't been able to dig up the money to get him any farther.

"Seems to me I did hear something about a hockey game tonight," he said roguishly, and the boy grinned.

"You can't kid me, Mr. Kelsey. I guess we're gonna lose the best right-winger we've ever had in Wheelsburg after you get a peek at Tim."

The boy paused, then brightened up. "I dunno how we'll get along without him, but I was sayin' to Al, the clerk, just the other day: 'We'll never be able to keep a high-class player like Tim here,' I said. 'The big teams will have scouts lookin' him over and they'll sign him up quicker'n scat.' Yessir, that's just what I told him."

"He's pretty good, is he?" Mr. Kelsey was beginning to see possibilities in the situation.

"Good! Listen—"

The bellhop went into a rhapsody. To hear him tell it, Tim Cardigan was the greatest professional hockey prospect at large. He was smarter than a fox, faster than a rabbit, and had a shot that made goalies turn pale with terror.

When the boy finally departed, still chanting the praises of the phenomenal Cardigan, the erstwhile scout for the Chiefs got into his neatly creased pants, whistling.

The sun was shining again. Tim Cardigan was probably terrible. Most of these small-town marvels were.

"But just the same," muttered Skates Kelsey, taking his last clean shirt from his grip, "I'm sayin' right here and now that the kid belongs in the big time. He's a wow. And I've never even seen him yet."

Bland, portly and respectable once more in the freshly pressed suit, he prepared to descend for dinner. No man without a nickel in his pocket could sign a dinner cheque with a grander flourish than Skates Kelsey.

At the door, however, he paused. Then he went back to the desk and notepaper. The dining room waitress, he was sure, would appreciate an autograph of Dave McKenna, the Chief goalie, instead of a mere cash tip.

• • •

IT WAS JUST a routine schedule game between Wheelsburg and Blueberry Bay, but Tim Cardigan's hands were trembling as he laced up his hockey boots in the tiny dressing room that night.

He was a lanky youth, tough as whipcord, with ink-black hair and a good-natured mouth. Ordinarily, the preparations for a hockey contest found him relaxed, taking it easy; but tonight he was shaking. A pro scout would be in the rink, watching him!

That seemed hard to believe. A pro scout in Wheelsburg!

"It's your big chance, lad," said his father, Dennis Cardigan, sole proprietor of the Wheelsburg Garage. "You play the best you know how. They don't send scouts all the way up here for nothin'."

Dennis Cardigan straightened up on the bench beside his son and bestowed a wide grin on the boys in the dressing room.

"By gorry, he could do worse than sign up the lot of you."

Tim tightened up a lace. "Maybe it's just talk."

"No," declared his father. "I heard it with me own ears from Al, the clerk at the Central House. It's Skates Kelsey. And well I remember the name; one of the finest defencemen in the country in his day. He gave young Pete Barr an autygraph of Charlie Warner."

"I saw it myself." piped up the goalie. "And Minnie, the dining-room girl. He gave her one of Dave McKenna, goalie for the Chiefs."

"And why shouldn't the Chiefs send a scout up to look at you?" demanded old Dennis. "Them big teams are lookin' for new blood all the time."

"How would he ever hear about me?"

"They'd hear about a good hockey player if he was playin' with a Eskimo team on an ice cake in Hudson Bay."

Tim stood up, straight and long-limbed. He reached for his stick and flexed it on the floor. He didn't seem excited, but he was. He tried to keep from thinking of what it would mean if a big-league scout actually saw him and liked him; if he actually landed a contract with a pro team.

Tim tried to put the dizzying prospect out of his head. It wouldn't do to count on it. Maybe the man wasn't a scout at all. And maybe he, Tim, wouldn't measure up to big-league standards, anyway.

"There's a big difference between the hockey we play here in Wheelsburg," he reminded the gang, "and the hockey they play in Madison Square Garden or the Forum."

"And where do you think they got the fellows who play in Madison Square Garden and the Forum?" demanded Dad Cardigan. "From small towns just like Wheelsburg. You just hop out there, me lad, and put Wheelsburg on the map!"

• • •

FOR TWENTY YEARS, the Wheelsburg rink had looked as if it might collapse at any moment—and for twenty years it had continued to fool everyone.

The roof had been propped up with so many assorted beams, timbers and scantlings that visitors always said you could identify a Wheelsburg hockey fan anywhere by his limber neck, developed by dodging his head around timbers while watching Wheelsburg hockey matches.

But Wheelsburg hockey fans didn't mind a touch of inconvenience or even danger with their sports fare. Every game found the ramshackle old rink crowded.

When the roof caved in—and Wheelsburg fans all agreed that only a miracle was holding it up—they gambled on the probability that the event would take place when there was no game in progress.

Tim batted the puck around in workout with his teammates at one end of the ice, while the Blueberry Bay outfit got the kinks out of their systems in the opposite goal area. Tim's kid brother Mike, who subbed on defence, skated alongside.

"There he is—sittin' behind the rail just this side of the

penalty box!" said Mike in a high state of excitement. "The red-faced guy in the derby."

The reference to the hue of Skates Kelsey's complexion was unnecessary. He was wearing the only derby there; the only derby in Wheelsburg, for that matter.

Tim cast a glance in the direction of the great Kelsey. So that stout little man over there had the power to lift a youngster out of the monotony and obscurity of a small town and thrust him into the glamour and fame of big-time hockey!

"Golly!" he said, and tried to keep calm. He didn't dare build up any hopes.

As Skates Kelsey watched the rangy Wheelsburg forward in workout, his agile brain was busy. Mr. Kelsey's immediate problem was to pay his hotel bill and get transportation back to the city. As to how this was to be managed, short of risking jail, he had no particular scruples.

"I watch this kid do his stuff," communed Skates Kelsey with himself. "Then I phone Harron that I've discovered a natural and signed him for a tryout. Harron will be scared of missing something, and he'll send transportation for both of us."

He knew just what to expect of Tim Cardigan. A small-town hockey player who looked good against small-town competition. He had seen hundreds of them. Take them out of their own class and they become ordinary.

But the Wheelsburg team and the outfit from Blueberry Bay hadn't been playing for five minutes before Skates Kelsey was sitting up very straight and blinking.

Tim Cardigan could skate. Plenty of hockey players could skate—they all could, of course—but there is skating and *skating*. This was the real stuff, the real McCoy!

Kelsey saw that, the first time the lanky winger took the trip down the boards.

Cardigan had taken a pass at the blue line from one of his defencemen. And then he broke. No windup. He simply broke from a standing start, and his journey down that right lane was a thing of beauty. The long legs ate up ice at every stride, and yet there seemed to be no extra effort. Tim Cardigan just loped down there like a greyhound, and when he crossed the blue line, his pass to centre was just a flick of the wrists.

The Blueberry defenceman got set with shoulders, knee, and stick as Tim Cardigan skimmed straight toward him. He was ready.

Kelsey groaned.

"Why, that's no way to go in," gasped Skates Kelsey. And when the defenceman cut loose with that bodycheck, he looked to see Tim Cardigan knocked kicking.

But at the last split second, as the defenceman lunged, lanky Cardigan just wasn't there. He was around and in there like a gust of wind, with the defenceman clattering to the ice. And he picked up the forward pass from his centre, strolled in, and poked the puck just inside the corner of the post as if there was no goalie doing a jumping jack act inside the cage.

It all looked so simple and natural and easy that Kelsey was sure the Wheelsburg fans didn't appreciate it.

For all that, the Blueberry Bay players weren't top-notchers; they were strong and heavy, good checkers, and their goalie was no slouch. It takes art to beat any goalie single-handed, without lifting the puck off the ice, and make it look soft.

"So!" mused Skates Kelsey, with tingling spine. "Where has this kid been all my life?"

The Blueberry team, saddened by past experience, no doubt, had assigned a tough, red-headed husky to left wing, under obvious instructions to do no rushing whatever; to do nothing but hang on to Tim Cardigan.

It was fun to watch Cardigan handle this watchdog. How he faded away from butt ends and bodychecks, how his stickhandling tied the left-winger into knots. As a matter of fact, the whole Blueberry team paid special attention to the lanky lad in the way of roughing it up, loudly encouraged by a small delegation of supporters; but you can't smash a phantom with a cross-check.

"Yes, sir," breathed Kelsey. "Regular ghost, that's what he is."

It was Cardigan's footwork that did it, he decided finally. The boy might have been born with skates on. Kelsey had never seen anyone who could go faster on a straight rush, who could break quicker in any direction, who could feint and shift and sidestep with such deceptive ease.

Cardigan never seemed to be trying particularly hard. But when there was a pass to his wing, he was always there to take it. When the Wheelsburg team were storming in around the Blueberry net, and Cardigan seemed to be loafing around outside the thick of the battle as an onlooker, there would be a swift, sudden swoop and he would be in there to collar a loose puck before anyone else had noticed the opening—and every time for a shot on goal.

Easy shots, they looked. He seldom tried a shot from farther than ten feet out. Always he worked in close. And then, that quick flip, as if it didn't matter.

But Skates Kelsey knew just how the goalie dreaded

those tricky flips from close in—always headed toward an open corner! Much harder to block than the fast, deliberate high shots from outside, although those were the drives that set the crowd cheering.

When Cardigan went to the bench, and a sub went to the wing in his stead, the Blueberry team managed to make some headway. The score was 4–1 against them, but they swamped the Wheelsburg crew with a series of wild-eyed rushes that netted them a couple of goals.

Then Cardigan came back. He was evidently an old and painful story to the Blueberry Bay team. They tried to rough him out of the picture.

Skates Kelsey learned then that Cardigan wasn't yellow. He could take it.

"Just a one-man circus!" beamed Skates Kelsey.

This, he told himself, was the greatest break of his life.

"When Harron gets a look at that prize package, I'll not only get my job back, but darned if I won't hit him for a raise. And get it."

• • •

FOR ALL HIS numerous faults, Skates Kelsey was a good scout. He knew hockey and he knew hockey players.

During the rest of the game, he concentrated on Tim Cardigan, looked for every possible fault.

He saw many, but none that could not be corrected. Faults of inexperience. On the credit side of the ledger he satisfied himself that Tim Cardigan had speed to burn, that he made no waste motions, that he had the physique to stand up under heavy going.

Most important of all, Cardigan had the temperament of the good hockey player—and he had hockey brains.

"Give me hockey brains in a player," Kelsey always said, "and I don't care what else he's got. Even if he's one-legged, I'll take him ahead of the fancy stickhandler or speed artist every time."

Along about the middle of the third period, with the Wheelsburg team leading by five goals, Skates Kelsey was satisfied. He had stumbled upon that rarest of gems—a hockey natural. From long habit, however, he maintained a poker face. Talk contract to some of these youngsters, and they got big ideas about money right away.

"What do you think of him, Mr. Kelsey?" asked the rink manager, squeezing in beside him.

"We-ell!" he replied. "It's hard to say. The boy is pretty green, of course. I've seen worse."

The rink manager was disappointed. He had expected that Kelsey would he singing hymns of praise.

"We think Tim is pretty good."

"He looks good in that company. He's got plenty to learn, though."

Skates Kelsey knew all about the rapidity of news circulation in a small community. It is more thorough than radio and just as fast. It was all over the rink inside five minutes that the scout for the Chiefs didn't think Tim Cardigan was so hot, after all.

Tim Cardigan, on the Wheelsburg bench, heard it and his heart tumbled clear down into his boots.

Dennis Cardigan growled: "What's the matter with the man? Is he blind? Doesn't he know a hockey player when he sees one?"

Tim burned up the ice in the final five minutes and the crowd applauded him loyally. He flipped in two goals, got an assist for another, looked like a million dollars on skates. When the game was over, he trudged to the dressing room trying to pretend to himself that he hadn't really expected to impress the scout.

• • •

SKATES KELSEY, escorted by the rink manager, paid the dressing room a visit after the game. Beaming jovially, Mr. Kelsey slapped backs, shook hands, complimented the players on their victory, made himself on good terms with everyone.

Introduced to Tim he said, "You played a nice game out there tonight, kid."

Tim choked. "Thanks, Mr. Kelsey."

"How about trying out with the Chiefs?" asked Kelsey calmly.

The room swam in front of Tim's eyes. Resigned to failure, he couldn't believe his ears for a moment. Then he blurted, "Why . . .why, you're not kidding, are you? Do you think I'm good enough?"

Kelsey shrugged. "That's up to the management. I send them a player and they give him a tryout." Then Skates Kelsey was fishing a folded sheet of paper from his pocket and handing it to Tim.

"This isn't a contract. But it gives me first call on your hockey services. Doesn't affect your amateur standing. Sign it, and I'll take you down for that tryout as soon as you can get ready."

The other players were squeaking with excitement. Dennis Cardigan reached over and took the paper from his son.

"I'll just read this over, me boy." He scanned the page carefully. "It doesn't say anything here about who pays Tim's fare to the city."

"Why, we do, naturally," Skates Kelsey assured him blithely. "All he has to do is sign that paper and we look after everything."

Dad Cardigan gave the paper back to Tim. "You can sign it, son."

Tim signed. The players cheered. It was all over Wheelsburg in ten minutes that Tim Cardigan had been snapped up by the big league Chiefs at a fabulous salary and would be playing right wing for the team within a week. Wheelsburg was on the map.

But while Tim was walking home on air, dizzy with the prospect of fame and fortune ahead of him, with Dad Cardigan and young Mike strutting beside him as proud as a pair of peacocks in his reflected glory, Skates Kelsey was having a bad five minutes on the long-distance telephone, at ninety cents a minute, charged against his hotel bill.

"But listen, Harron, I tell you this boy is a natural. He's got the makings of one of the best right-wingers in hockey, and you know how scarce they are. And I've got him for the Chiefs. All signed up."

"Baloney! You got my telegram, didn't you?"

"Yes, but—"

"Well, it still goes."

"Have a heart!" begged Skates, desperately. "I tell you this is serious. If you pass up this player—"

"Listen," said his boss, coldly. "You're in a jam up there, and I'm glad of it. Serves you right. You figure you can give me a song-and-dance about some punk and I'll send you the dough to bring him down here."

"You know I wouldn't try to play a trick like that on you."

"I know damned well that's just the trick you're trying to pull right now. I know just how your mind works. If this guy was any good, we'd have heard of him before now. Nix!"

Skates Kelsey was horrified. "You can't do this to me!" he bleated. "I've got the kid all signed up."

"Then unsign him," snapped Harron. "I don't want any part of him, or you either."

• • •

THE RECEIVER CLICKED smartly in Skates Kelsey's ear. He was sweating as he stumbled out of the phone booth at the back of the hotel lobby.

He hadn't dared put the call through collect, for fear it would be refused, which would have made Al, the hotel clerk, highly suspicious. As it was, he hoped the girl on night duty at the local switchboard had resisted any temptation to listen in.

He flopped into a leather chair by the window and stared moodily out at the snow-covered road. He had started this as a gag, and now that it was on the level, he was hogtied. There he was, with a superdooper of a right-winger in his pocket, and he might as well be in China, for all the good it was going to do him.

Skates Kelsey had wriggled out of many a tight corner in his time, but for once it looked as if he was stymied. Was this what a man got for reforming? The minute he stepped on the straight and narrow path, fate socked him with a sandbag.

His thoughts darted this way and that, like trapped mice. Once the townspeople got wise to the true state of affairs, they would chase him clear to the next county.

"I've got to get that kid down to the city," mused Kelsey, in desperation. "One look at him and Harron will take everything back."

But how to get out? A big-league scout couldn't ask a prospect to ride side-door Pullman, with a wrathful hotel manager shrieking vengeance for an unpaid hotel bill.

And so Skates Kelsey sat immersed in gloom.

• • •

WHILE IN THE Cardigan kitchen, Dad Cardigan sucked at his pipe and gazed proudly at his eldest son. Ma Cardigan, brushing away an occasional tear, was going over Tim's socks and underwear.

"Did the man say what pay you'd be getting?" she asked.

Tim shook his head. "He didn't talk money. But if they sign me, I'll probably get about fifty a week to start."

"Holy oats!" breathed young Mike, in awe.

"You'll be drawin' down seven or eight thousand dollars a season before you're much older," predicted Dad Cardigan. "Smart men like Mr. Kelsey don't waste their time on players that ain't worth it."

"This time tomorrow night," said Ma Cardigan, her voice proud and sad, "you'll probably be on your way to the city. In a Pullman car, maybe."

• • •

BY MORNING, after a sleepless night, Skates Kelsey was still racking his brains for an idea. Most of the notions that had occurred to him revolved about rubber cheques, and he knew the railway ticket office wouldn't take a cheque, anyway.

But at breakfast, where he presented his usual blandly confident front, an idea was given to him. By none other than Tim Cardigan himself, who peeped into the dining room and came humbly over to his table.

"Sit down, son! Sit down!" beamed Kelsey. "Had your breakfast? Well, have a cup of coffee, anyway. Minnie, a cup of coffee for Tim. What's on your mind, boy? All ready for the trip?"

Tim sat down. "Did you . . . did you want me to leave right away, Mr. Kelsey? Today?"

"Well, the sooner the better, of course," replied Kelsey, wondering what was in the wind and hoping Tim wouldn't want to leave for a week. "What's up?"

"It's this way. Mr. Parkes, the rink manager, got a telegram this morning from a barnstorming outfit that's been playing games in the West, and they'd like a game here tomorrow night."

"And you'd like to play?"

"Well, it isn't that so much as the fact that Mr. Parkes and some of the boys talked it over and they figured it would be a nice idea to make it a benefit game—for me, so

I'd have a little spending money."

At the magic word "money," Skates Kelsey sat up, eyes agleam. An answer to prayer! Why hadn't he thought of it himself?

"Why, naturally, my boy, you can't miss your own benefit game!" he boomed jovially. "I'll stay over myself. And you tell the boys I want to help. I'll face the puck. Why, I'll even sell tickets!"

"Would you? Gosh!" Tim was overwhelmed.

No doubt about it, this Skates Kelsey was a swell fellow. Imagine, a famous man like Kelsey actually offering to sell tickets for a hockey benefit. The fans would fight for the privilege of buying them.

"I'll be only too glad to help," promised Mr. Kelsey fervently.

There wasn't any dishonesty in Kelsey's make-up, to the extent that he wanted to lay hands on the benefit money for himself. All he wanted was ready cash, which would certainly be returned to Tim Cardigan just as soon as the Chiefs' manager saw him and realized that Kelsey had not been exaggerating his worth at all.

It was for Cardigan's own good, Kelsey told himself. To what better use could the benefit money be devoted than to guarantee Cardigan his tryout? Kelsey wasn't crooked. Just desperate.

All that afternoon, as soon as the tickets were ready at the Wheelsburg printing shop, Skates Kelsey worked for the cause. All he needed, he figured, was a miserable seventy-five dollars to cover transportation, berths, meals and hotel bill. But with tickets selling at thirty-five cents each and the barnstorming team—the Black Bombers by name—demanding a sixty-forty split of the gross, it would take some doing.

Feverishly, he plunged into the business of getting rid of tickets. "Gimme a couple of hundred—three hundred!" he told Tim.

"Good gosh, Mr. Kelsey, the fellows figured that if you even sold forty or fifty—"

"Chicken feed. I'll show you how to sell tickets. Does this town send a player up to the big time every day?"

• • •

AS A TICKET SALESMAN, Kelsey was a howling success. Any customer who sought the honour of shaking the great Skates Kelsey's hand at the cost of buying one ticket had a rude jolt in store for him.

"*One* ticket!" Kelsey would exclaim with mock horror, taking the sting out of it with a hearty chuckle. "This is a benefit. You can use extra tickets. Give 'em away, keep 'em for souvenirs."

Anyone who tried to buy one or even two tickets and was foolish enough to produce a dollar bill in payment discovered that Mr. Kelsey never had any change, but he had lots more tickets.

"You've got the finest right-winger in hockey right here in Wheelsburg. He's gonna make your town famous. Don't you appreciate him? Well then, show him, by making this benefit a sellout," he chanted.

Skates Kelsey bullied Wheelsburg into buying tickets until it hurt, and made them like it.

The money rolled in. By noon next day, Skates Kelsey's pockets sagged with the weight of one hundred and forty dollars in cash, with more to come at the box office. How was he going to hang onto seventy-five dollars of this without stirring up unworthy suspicions?

If Tim Cardigan balked at a confidential suggestion that Skates Kelsey should take charge of his affairs and look after his money for him—considering Mr. Kelsey's vast experience and in view of all he had done to put the benefit over with a bang—the youngster would be either a good deal shrewder or a lot more ungrateful than Kelsey expected.

"Yes, sir," mused Kelsey. "A man with brains can always land on his feet somehow."

Everything was lovely.

And then the Black Bombers arrived on the afternoon train, along with a bundle of daily papers from the nearest city and a small, gloomy traveller for a wholesale meat firm.

The Bombers, the newspapers, and the traveller—who checked in at the Central House modestly as R. B. Jones— were destined to affect the fortunes of Skates Kelsey and Tim Cardigan.

Kelsey was in the hotel lobby when the Bombers arrived. They came trooping in, a dozen husky young fellows led by a swarthy six-footer named Dave Carter. And the moment Kelsey laid eyes on the Bomber chieftain, he sagged like a deflated tire and uttered a moan of pained astonishment.

As for Carter, when he recognized Skates Kelsey, his mouth opened in surprise. Then he bristled. They knew each other of old, and no love had ever been lost between them. Bitter enemies and deadly rivals they were, for Carter, too, had been a big-leaguer in the days when Skates Kelsey was in his prime.

The feud between them had been historic from the day Kelsey dumped Carter into the boards during the first game in which they ever tangled. The present crookedness of Carter's nose was a memento of that occasion.

Carter recognized his old enemy. "Hello, Cheapskates," he grunted out of the side of his mouth, using the salutation that had started many an ice battle in the old days. "Didn't expect to find you here. This your hometown?"

Kelsey shook his head. He was doing a lot of fast thinking. He had never cared for the sight of Dave Carter at any time; but just now, the arrival of his most bitter enemy promised to be disastrous, for Dave Carter was an unofficial scout for the Red Wings!

"I'm here on business," Kelsey said shortly.

"Had to go to work for a living?" inquired Carter. "Whatcha been doing since the Chiefs fired you?"

Skates Kelsey stiffened. Everyone in the lobby, including Al, the clerk, and half a dozen natives of Wheelsburg, had heard that crack. It created a sensation.

"You're nuts," he answered. "I'm still scouting for the Chiefs."

"Sez you!" snapped Carter. "It's in all the papers. I read it on the train this morning."

He whipped a newspaper out of his pocket, flipped it

open to the sports section and thrust the page under Kelsey's nose.

"Who's lyin', Cheapskates?" he demanded. "Me, you, or the newspaper?"

Dully, Skates Kelsey read the item under a city dateline:

CHIEFS DROP SCOUT

Rumoured as a possibility in hockey circles for some time, the retirement of Skates Kelsey, former pro star, as scout for the Chiefs, was definitely announced by President Ben Harron of the Chiefs today. Foster Denning, publicity representative of the club, will finish out the season as scout and leaves tonight on a swing through the East to watch leading amateur teams in action.

Skates Kelsey flushed and swallowed hard. For once, his nerve was shattered.

"Who's lyin'?" repeated Carter.

"You are," said Kelsey, in a hoarse voice, and turned away. "I'm still scoutin' for the Chiefs. I don't care what the papers say."

Inside five minutes, every newspaper that arrived on the afternoon train had been snapped up. The news was all over town.

Dave Carter was explaining to Al, the hotel clerk, and a growing crowd of Wheelsburgians that Skates Kelsey was a booze artist, a gambler, and a bum, particularly untrustworthy in money matters, and that it was a wonder the Chiefs had ever put up with him at all.

Tim Cardigan was staggered when he heard the story. Did this mean that he wasn't going to get his tryout with the Chiefs after all? Worried, he talked it over with his equally worried father in the garage office, and into the conference strode Parkes, the rink manager. Parkes was in a sweat.

"The fair thing to do is for us to go and ask Mr. Kelsey what's what, and hear what he has to say for himself," suggested Dennis Cardigan.

"I don't care what he has to say for himself," snapped Parkes. "He's got a lot of money belonging to us from those tickets he sold, and I'm taking no chances."

"Begorra!" said Dennis, turning pale. "If he's a crook, he may be plannin' on skipping out."

They lost no time in hustling over to the hotel. To their vast relief, they found that Skates Kelsey had not skipped out, but was in his room. And Mr. Kelsey, who had recovered some of his nerve, was ready for them.

"All nonsense!" he assured them smoothly. "Why, I was talking to Mr. Harron just last night on long distance. Told him I was bringing Tim down with me."

"But it said in the paper—" objected Dennis Cardigan.

"Must be some mistake," declared Skates Kelsey firmly. "In the first place, they couldn't dismiss me without notice. Doesn't a season's contract mean anything?"

They began to weaken. Skates Kelsey talked fast and with conviction. Inside five minutes, they were apologizing to him. Even if the Chiefs did want to fire him when he got back to the city, said Mr. Kelsey, it wouldn't stand in the way of Tim Cardigan's tryout.

But it was Parkes, the rink manager, who had the last word. "I'm mighty glad we've got the truth about this, Mr. Kelsey," he said. "We were afraid, for a minute, that maybe Tim wouldn't get going south after all. By the way, could I have your returns for all them tickets you sold?"

Skates Kelsey winced. The blow had fallen. "Why, certainly. Certainly," he replied. "I'll drop in at the box office tonight and fix it up."

Mr. Parkes drew him over to the window. "I'd just as soon have the money now, if you don't mind, Mr. Kelsey. You see, instead of givin' Tim the cash," he whispered confidentially, "we made up our minds to buy him a watch and a suitcase."

Skates Kelsey took it like a man. He coughed up. There was a slight discrepancy between the number of tickets he claimed to have sold and the number of tickets he said he had left, as against the number of tickets originally given him; but, at that, he didn't manage to hold out more than a dollar and a half.

When his visitors left, he slumped down on the bed. "Licked!" he groaned. "Licked to a frazzle! And when Dave Carter gets a look at this Cardigan boy in action tonight, it won't be the Chiefs who'll sign him. Carter will sign him for the Red Wings, sure as shootin'."

• • •

MR. R. B. JONES, the meat salesman, was a quiet, businesslike little man with a tight mouth and a close-cropped moustache. He visited Wheelsburg's two butcher shops that afternoon, explained that he was substituting for the man who usually covered the territory, took a few orders and kept his ears open.

He heard a good deal of hockey talk, and apparently it interested him so much that he decided to stay over for the game, although he could have gone out on the six-o'clock local.

When Tim Cardigan came down to the rink that night, he was all set to show his fans and friends in Wheelsburg that their confidence in him hadn't been misplaced. He was rarin' to go, itching to play the sort of game that they would remember. This would be his night!

He was flabbergasted when Skates Kelsey, who came in looking as bland and jovial as ever, took him off into a corner of the dressing room and said, "Tim, I'm going to ask you to do something for me. Maybe it won't be easy. Maybe you won't like it. But for the sake of your own future, I want you to do it."

Tim blinked. "Why, sure. What do you want me to do, Mr. Kelsey?"

"I want you to take it easy out there tonight, Tim."

"Take it easy? Why, gosh, this is my benefit, Mr. Kelsey. This is my send-off. They'll be expectin' me to cut loose with everything I've got."

"And that's just what you're not to do. This barnstorming team is a rough bunch, Tim. I don't want you to run any chances of being hurt."

"Shucks, they'll never touch me."

"Listen. Do you know that this fellow Carter, who manages the Bombers, is hooked up with the Red Wings? Well, he is. I've been hearing a few things," continued Kelsey mysteriously. "If you came out of this game with a charley horse or a wrenched shoulder or a cracked rib—"

"They wouldn't deliberately try to get me."

"Well, if anything happened to you, I couldn't take you down for a tryout. And the Red Wings aren't anxious to see the Chiefs strengthened at right wing at this stage of the season, my boy. Think it over."

Tim thought it over. He nodded slowly.

"What's more," declared Kelsey impressively, "I don't want the other pro teams to know anything about how good you are until the time comes. If Carter can report to the Red Wings that I'm making a mistake in signing you up, so much the better."

Skates Kelsey made it sound very convincing. His real motive, of course, was to forestall the possibility that his old enemy, Carter, might steal this prize right-winger. Kelsey didn't care if Cardigan stayed in Wheelsburg the rest of his life.

"If I can't get him, I'll be darned if I'll let Carter have him," he told himself.

"I've never played a game in my life that I didn't do my best," said Tim Cardigan. "All my friends will be out there hollerin' for me. They won't know what to make of it. But if you think it's best, Mr. Kelsey—"

Skates Kelsey slapped him warmly on the shoulder. "I knew you'd be sensible about it, Tim. It's a hard thing to do,

but pro hockey is tricky business. I'm giving you the sound-
est advice I know."

• • •

WHEN TIM CARDIGAN skated out for the game with the barnstorming Bombers that night, a thunderous roar went up
from the fans who jammed every corner of the rink.

Every eye in the building was on him. It was his night.
But three pairs of eyes were fixed on him with more than
ordinary interest.

Dave Carter, manager of the Bombers and unofficial
scout for the Red Wings, had heard all about Tim Cardigan
that afternoon—all about how Cardigan was leaving for a
tryout with the Chiefs, and Carter was saying, "If the kid is
any good, I'll push Kelsey out of the picture so fast it'll
make his head swim."

Skates Kelsey, sitting in a rail seat morosely, with his hat
brim down over his eyes, was wondering how he was going
to get out of town. Broke again, there wasn't a chance in
the world that he could keep his promise to bring Cardigan
south for a tryout.

"Anyhow, I've fixed it so Carter won't want to steal him.
And maybe if I can get back home and talk to Harron,

they'll send for the kid."

Mr. R. B. Jones, the meat salesman, sitting two rows behind Kelsey, watched Tim Cardigan skate over and take his position. And R. B. Jones said to himself, "Kelsey, you're a cold-blooded crook. Kidding that boy into thinking he's going to be a big-leaguer when you know he hasn't a chance. Making a fool of him right in his own hometown."

Mr. Jones was sorry for Tim Cardigan.

Small boys along the rail near Tim Cardigan were yelling shrilly, "You show 'em, Tim!" as the referee faced off the puck. "Show these barnstormers some big-league hockey, Tim!"

Those eager shouts of encouragement didn't make Tim feel so good. He felt that he was double-crossing those youngsters. But Skates Kelsey was giving him his big chance; Skates Kelsey wouldn't have asked him to take it easy in this game without good reason.

The Bombers played in an Eastern league with little opposition and a short schedule, and their barnstorming trip had been arranged to give them extra games and a variety of opposition.

A good team of hockey tramps, they were tired from their journey and were taking this exhibition lightly—with the exception of Leask, their left-winger, who had been told by Dave Carter to go out there and extend Tim Cardigan to the limit.

On the very first play, when Leask took a pass from his centre and broke down the boards, Tim took a hard smash into the fence when he tried to stop the fast-travelling Bomber wing. He scrambled up and went pelting after Leask, stole the puck from him inside the blue line and whirled back. The crowd roared in expectation of a Wheelsburg attack.

But Tim remembered what Kelsey had told him. He put on the brakes at mid-ice and went in cautiously, passed to centre. The Bomber centre raced in fast to intercept the pass and wheeled away on the attack.

There were a few murmurs from the Wheelsburg fans. Their hero, Tim Cardigan, hadn't looked so good on that play.

But they comforted themselves with assurances that Tim would soon settle down to business, and then it would take the whole Bomber team to hold him.

Five minutes passed. Ten minutes. The Wheelsburg players kept feeding the puck to Tim, as they always did, depending on him to lead the rushes into enemy territory.

But the old speed, the old brilliance of stickhandling and footwork, the heady playmaking—these were missing.

He moved in fits and starts, his checking was cautious and clumsy, he didn't seem to be sure of himself.

The truth of the matter was that Tim Cardigan didn't know how to play anything but his usual game. Trying to hold himself in and to take it easy, he floundered.

Leask, his check, ran wild on the wing and tore through for a couple of goals before the period was half over.

Half a dozen times, Tim forgot himself and ripped into the game with some of his old fire; but just when the fans thought they were seeing the Tim Cardigan they knew, these flare-ups petered out and he settled down to that cagy, wooden style of play so foreign to him.

The rest of the Wheelsburg team didn't know what to make of it. They were so accustomed to Tim's leadership that now they were utterly at sea. Dennis Cardigan, manager of the team, was so flustered that he kept sending out substitutes repeatedly, trying to get a combination that would click.

But nothing clicked, except the Bombers' attack.

The Bombers came down on swift, stabbing two- and three-man rushes that swept neatly over the blue line again and again. Two more goals were chalked up along with Leask's tallies, and they came so easily that the Bombers began laying back a little. After all, this was only an exhibition game, and it wouldn't be good policy to tramp all over the home team.

"That guy a hockey player!" exclaimed Dave Carter, when the period ended and he had seen all of Tim Cardigan that he considered necessary. "He's terrible. Cheapskate Kelsey was trying to pull a fast one, all right."

Behind him, he could hear the fans grumbling.

"What's the matter with Tim?"

"He's away off his game."

"Never saw him play worse."

But those remarks didn't impress Carter. He had heard that sort of talk before.

• • •

TIM DIDN'T HAVE much to say for himself in the dressing room between periods. He knew better than anyone else that he was giving a terrible exhibition, but he didn't know how to make it look any smoother without disobeying Skates Kelsey.

"You feelin' all right tonight, son?" ventured Dennis Cardigan.

"Sure, I'm all right."

"Don't seem to be playin' your usual game, kind of."

"I'm not taking any chances on getting hurt in an exhibition game, with a pro tryout waiting for me," flared Tim.

"Yeah. I know, but just the same—"

Dennis Cardigan didn't finish what he wanted to say. It wasn't like Tim to give hockey anything but his best, whether the going was rough or easy.

Tim put in a miserable twenty minutes in the second period. Leask, the Bomber winger, tried to stir him up, rammed him against the boards a couple of times, mixed it up with him in the corners, for Leask sensed something wrong, and he was wondering if this Wheelsburg forward had anything after all. But Tim took his bumping meekly and began steering clear of Leask whenever he could.

It developed into a sloppy game. The Wheelsburg team couldn't do anything right, and the Bombers just coasted. The Wheelsburg fans gaped, astounded at the spectacle of Tim Cardigan, whom they had come to honour, backing away from bodychecks and generally turning in the most futile game they had ever seen him play.

The score at the end of the second period was 6–0 in favour of the Bombers. And when the mayor of Wheelsburg came out onto the ice in the rest period and called Tim out for the presentation, the applause wasn't as spirited as it might have been.

The mayor presented Tim with a gold watch and a fine new suitcase, which Tim accepted with the air of one who didn't deserve anything of the sort.

And when the mayor spoke of Wheelsburg's high hopes for "this sterling young athlete who will soon make the name of Wheelsburg famous when he takes his place with the finest hockey players in the world," there did seem to be a doubtful note in the cheering that followed.

Dave Carter laughed out loud.

• • •

MR. R. B. JONES, the meat salesman, tight-lipped with anger, pushed his way down through the crowd and wedged himself into a space beside Skates Kelsey.

"A dirty trick, Kelsey," he said quietly. "A mean, lowdown trick to play. How do you think the kid is going to live this down?"

Skates Kelsey turned slowly and stared at Mr. Jones. "Whaddaya mean?"

"You know as well as I do that the kid hasn't any more chance of catching on with the Chiefs than I have. How's he going to feel when you duck out of town and he finds that it was all a gag and that there isn't even a tryout in it for him?"

"And what makes you so sure it's a gag, mister?"

"Because I know hockey and hockey players," snapped Jones. "Because I got a wire from Harron yesterday, asking me to stop off here and look at this find of yours."

Kelsey's eyes bulged. "You—Harron sent you?"

"Harron thought you were pulling a fast one, but he didn't want to take any chances. He told me to look at the kid and send him on down for a tryout if it was on the level. And to send you along with him."

"But listen," spluttered Kelsey, "you haven't seen him go. He's been under wraps. On account of maybe Carter tryin' to grab him for the Wings."

"Don't give me that," replied Jones, scornfully. "Think I was born yesterday? I'm Jones, of the Jones Packing Co. Maybe you've heard of my team, the Packers, one of the best industrial teams in the country. I've had a box seat at the Chiefs' games for five years. I don't have to look at a punk for more than two periods to know he's a punk."

Mr. Jones turned away from the frantic Kelsey. "I've seen all I care to see of this game. Too bad you gypped yourself out of that ticket back home, smart guy," he flung back.

"Wait a minute!" bleated Kelsey.

But the fans were returning to their seats as the teams came back on the ice. As Kelsey floundered in pursuit, he was buffeted this way and that by the crowd. By the time he reached the head of the aisle, he had lost Jones in the confusion.

• • •

JUST BEFORE Tim Cardigan left the dressing room, he took a last look at the fine new suitcase and at the magnificent gold watch the people of Wheelsburg had given him. He got all choked up when he thought of the faith and affection those gifts represented.

"Look after 'em for me, will you, Bill?" he asked Parkes, the rink manager.

"I'll lock them in the office." The manager's voice seemed strained.

Tim could sense that Parkes was disappointed in him. This benefit game was to have been a triumph for Tim.

"I'll make it up to 'em," Tim promised himself silently as he skated out, "when I'm playing with the Chiefs."

And yet, as the third period got under way, he couldn't help feeling that he was making a poor return to Wheelsburg right now. The watch and the club bag were from his hometown folks, to remind him always of their loyalty. And he was letting them down.

Leask, of the Bombers, was coming down the boards slowly with the puck. Impulsively, Tim stepped in, his stick flashed out and back as he hooked the puck from Leask's stick. Leask whipped in again and bumped him; bumped him hard and savagely. Tim lost his footing and went down. Leask snapped up the puck, grinning, and streaked away.

"Aw, Tim!" shrilled a youngster along the rail. "Don't let him get away with that."

Tim was on his feet. Maybe Kelsey was a smart hockey man, but he didn't know everything. You didn't have to let your own crowd down and let yourself be kicked around by a second-rate barnstormer as the price of getting into the big time. If that was the price, he'd rather stay in Wheelsburg.

Tim lit out after Leask, caught up with him inside the blue line, harried him, chased him over to the boards, into a corner, and wound up by intercepting Leask's attempted pass to the Bomber centre.

There was a scattering of applause from some of the Wheelsburg crowd. So far as Tim Cardigan was concerned, that applause was like a spark to gunpowder.

"To heck with Kelsey! If he doesn't like it, he can lump it. I'd rather stay in Wheelsburg and know they like me, than make the big time and know I let Wheelsburg down."

He swooped out from behind the net, travelling fast,

and cut back to his own wing. For the first time that evening he let himself go. He hit the blue line flying. The Bombers, who had long since decided that Tim Cardigan had neither speed nor ability, were caught flat-footed.

A pass to his own centre as he crossed the Bomber blue line. He shifted around the defence, but the Wheelsburg centre's pass was short. Tim had to swoop back for it. He beat a defenceman to the disk by an eyelash.

The Bombers were all back now, trying to break it up, but he fenced and side-stepped his way through a maze of clashing sticks, trying to get in position for a shot.

He lost the puck, dove after it, regained it again and in the same movement saw an opening as a pair of struggling players lunged over from in front of the net. Tim let go with a flick of the wrists. The puck bounced into the twine off the toe of the goalie's boot.

Wheelsburg had something to cheer for at last. Wheelsburg came to its feet with a mighty roar. That was what they had been waiting for.

Tim Cardigan was tingling with pleasure as he skated back with the loyal cheers of the hometown folks in his ears. Why, he'd rather have Wheelsburg cheers than the applause of all the crowds in the big time! He caught a glimpse of Dave Carter's astonished face as Carter gaped at him from the Bomber bench.

"Attaboy, Tim!" screeched one of the kids in the end balcony near the mechanical organ. "You were just foolin' 'em all the time!"

The Bombers thought it was just a flash in the pan. But after the faceoff, they learned different. Their centre man won the draw and tried to take the puck down, but Tim Cardigan swooped across from the wing, stick low on the ice, body crouched.

The Bomber centre figured Leask was wide open for a pass and he tried it. But the long Cardigan arm and the long Cardigan stick and the Cardigan speed broke up that effort.

Tim Cardigan's stick deflected the puck down the ice and then he was after it like a greyhound, darting through the gap between wing and centre.

He was thundering down on the defence while the Bomber forwards were still turning in their tracks. And this time, his savage shot from outside was a blistering high drive for the upper corner of the net.

And the goalie, who hadn't been worried by any real Cardigan shots for two periods, was just a fraction of a second too slow judging it. The puck was in the net before he could even make a play.

And then Wheelsburg really opened up and cheered!

The goal didn't matter; the score didn't matter. What mattered was that Tim Cardigan was honestly doing his stuff. They were still roaring when the referee faced off again. And when the Bombers pulled up their socks and pitched in to find an honest-to-goodness hockey game on their hands instead of a walk-over, the fur began to fly.

The Wheelsburg team rallied behind Tim Cardigan, who was flashing up and down that right lane as if trying to make up for lost time. He tied Leask into knots every time the Bomber wing tried to break away. He led Wheelsburg on rush after rush against the astonished visitors, the spearhead of the attack. He was a two-way player, able to bring the puck down and stop it coming back.

Dave Carter told his centre to help Leask stop the tornado that had broken out so surprisingly on the wing. And with two Bombers hanging onto him, Tim grinned and began feeding the puck to his uncovered centre. That paved the way for another rush.

At the halfway mark, with bumps aplenty being handed out, and the Bombers driven back on their heels, Tim Cardigan shook himself loose from two Bombers who were trying to bottle him up behind the Bomber net. He pulled out of it, shifted, waited for another Bomber to come in after him, and then he slipped a wide pass out to young Mike.

The way was wide open. Young Mike Cardigan jumped in like an owl after a mouse and banged it home for the third goal.

Wheelsburg went wild.

"By gosh, he was just kiddin' 'em along, all those first two periods!" declared Wheelsburg fans joyously.

And as the Wheelsburg team hit its stride again behind the flying Tim, the Bombers began to fade.

"You can't hold that one-man gang!" panted Leask, scrambling in for a rest. "What was the matter with him those other two periods? That's what I'd like to know."

"I'd like to know, too," grunted Dave Carter, his face cloudy.

He watched one of his defencemen try to slow Tim Cardigan up with a bodycheck and saw Cardigan fade away from it so neatly that the defenceman went sprawling. The goalie lunged out to make a stop, and hung onto the puck. The whistle blew for a faceoff.

Dennis Cardigan sent out his subs. But Tim waved the relief right-winger back.

"Beat it. I'm playin' the whole period!"

It was as if a great weight had been taken off his back. Tim Cardigan was playing his own game and he was going to pack as much of it into twenty minutes as he could.

As for Skates Kelsey, his face was gray and flabby as he stood near one of the exits. Kelsey was seeing the prize find of the season slipping out of his fingers.

"Yes, sir," muttered Kelsey, "the cat's outta the bag now. Carter will have him signed up before the night's out. And me, the guy who found him, without a thin dime to pay my hotel bill!"

Someone grabbed Kelsey's arm. "I don't often apologize to people," said a clipped, familiar voice. "Because I'm not often wrong. But this time—"

Kelsey looked down. Mr. R. B. Jones, pale and excited, was standing beside him.

"Holy cats!" yelled R. B. Jones suddenly. "If it hadn't been that there was such a crowd here that I couldn't find my way out, I'd have missed it! Under wraps, you said. I'll say he was under wraps! Why, that boy is the best right-wing prospect I've looked at in years!"

Skates Kelsey sagged with relief. "Yeah," he said weakly. "That's what I tried to tell Harron."

"Where's the nearest phone?" demanded R. B. Jones. "I'm gonna get Harron on long-distance right away. This time, we'll both tell him!"

ABOUT LESLIE McFARLANE

To young detectives worldwide, Leslie McFarlane was known under the pseudonyms Carolyn Keene, Roy Rockwood and, most famously, Franklin W. Dixon—author of The Hardy Boys series. McFarlane, who passed away in 1977, was one of the most successful Canadian writers of all time. Working for the *Stratemeyer Syndicate*, he penned twenty-one volumes of The Hardy Boys, initiated The Dana Girls series and wrote seven Dave Fearless novels. Aside from his work as The Hardy Boys author, McFarlane penned four novels, one hundred novelettes, two hundred short stories, and seventy-five television scripts. He also produced, directed and wrote fifty films for the National Film Board. McFarlane was nominated for an Academy Award for scripting the documentary drama *Herring Hunt* in 1953. He also worked in Hollywood as a writer for the television show *Bonanza* before returning to Canada where he worked on documentaries and comedies for the CBC. He passed away in 1977, at the age of seventy-five.